His Runaway Crush

Easter in Gilead
Book 3

HEATHER GRAY

EASTER IN GILEAD BOOKS

Her Unlikely Hero by Valerie Comer
Her Billionaire Benefactor by Elizabeth Maddrey
His Runaway Crush by Heather Gray

Cover design by Jess Mastorakos.

Published in the United States of America by Heather Gray.
    www.heathergraywriting.com

Publisher's Note: This novel is a work of fiction. Names and places are either products of the author's imagination or used fictitiously. All characters and events are fictional, and any similarity to people living or dead is coincidental.

in celebration of my Savior
I know redemption only because He lives.
in memory of my daughter
She made my world brighter and painted it with broad strokes
of vibrant color.
with pride in my son
He stretches my understanding of life, people, and God while
filling our home with music.
with gratitude for my husband
I'm glad we've been able to walk this path together.

The LORD is near to the brokenhearted and saves the crushed in spirit.
Psalm 34:18 (ESV)

1

——————

"Absolutely not." Dawson Bauer held onto his self-control with an iron grip. Only his metaphorical palms must have been sweaty because his hold was starting to slip.

The man across from him — whatever his name was — blinked before running a hand over his sparse white comb over. "It's in your contract."

"You're mistaken. I would have seen it, and I wouldn't have accepted the position here if that was the case."

The head of human resources at the Gilead Bible College patted the pockets of his tweed jacket before pulling out a pair of reading glasses and slipping them on. How they stayed there, balanced precariously as they were on the tip of the man's nose, was anybody's guess. He thumbed through the papers in the crisp manilla folder he'd been wielding when he'd walked into Dawson's office.

With a grunt, the older man set a copy of Dawson's employment contract on the desk and jabbed his finger at the section labeled *Special Events*. "It's right there."

Dawson was familiar with the section. It was his employment contract, after all. He'd read it before signing. Still, he could at least humor the HR guy. He scanned the section before looking up again. "See, it's exactly as I remember. There's nothing about…"

Wait a second. Dawson dropped his gaze back to the page. What was that…?

The Head of the College's Audio/Visual Department will oversee lighting and sound for the school's annual passion play. This includes but is not limited to all auditions, full dress rehearsals, and performances, and 80% of other (not full dress) rehearsals.

The force of the words pushed Dawson back in his chair. He looked up, stricken, his eyes searching out the watery grey ones peering at him over the top of those barely-holding-on reading glasses. "I don't remember seeing this."

The man pointed to the bottom of the page. "You initialed it."

"I never would have taken the job."

"Well, it's too late for that. You've signed a contract, and auditions start this afternoon, so you need to be there."

Dawson bit back the words he wanted to say. Though his grip was more aluminum than iron at the moment, he maintained enough self-control not to shout about just how much he hated Easter. Barely. Hating Easter wasn't the sort of thing that one ought to yell, especially when sitting in an office in the heart of Gilead Bible College.

The school produced a passion play each year. Auditions started in a few hours, and he had to be there.

Best first day on the job ever. Not.

"You don't want to be in breach of your contract." The older man's words weren't harsh, but his stare was one that probably had most grown men shaking in their boots.

Dawson wasn't most men, though, and his antipathy for

Easter outweighed his sense of self-preservation. "What happens if I refuse?"

"You might never get a job at a Christian college or university again."

The air whistled in its rush to leave his lungs. "You can't do that."

The man tidied the copy of Dawson's contract and slipped it back into his manilla folder. "I can. I'm not sure I would, but I absolutely can. Do not mistake my advanced years for weakness."

Helplessness morphed into a ball of smoldering rage in Dawson's gut. "Why not just cut me loose?"

An age-spotted hand patted down the combover again. "You're a man of your word, Dawson Bauer, and you gave us your word. Besides..." He rapped his knuckles against Dawson's gargantuan wooden desk. "God has plans for you here. Letting you off the hook would be going against Him, and I try not to do that."

On that cryptic note, the man slipped out the door, and Dawson was left staring at nothing as he contemplated the colossal mess into which he'd landed.

He hated Easter. Hated it. With the fire of a thousand burning suns.

Or, at least, he'd hated it for the first few years after...

Maybe he didn't hate it so much anymore. It was more like indifference with a side of loathing. Enough loathing to make him avoid all things Easter.

He was a believer, and he was faithful, but...

Easter had too many ugly memories tangled up with it. He'd never been able to separate the darkness of those memories from the joy he was supposed to feel each year as all of Christendom celebrated the resurrection.

How on earth was Dawson supposed to know what kind of setup the stage needed for auditions? Nobody had given him a clue, it was his first real day on campus, and he had no idea who was in charge of running this show.

He tugged a bag full of microphones off the shelf and let the equipment room's door slam behind him.

He dropped the bag on the edge of the stage before hopping up. After setting up a few mic stands and getting cables plugged in, he headed to the stairs at stage left. In his younger years, he might have vaulted off the stage. At the ripe old age of thirty, though, he considered his actions more carefully. Mostly. Besides, he was angry. Stomping down the stairs soothed his frayed nerves.

As he strode toward the sound booth at the back of the auditorium, movement caught his eye. A woman dragged two folded tables through a backlit staff-only door that was propped open. She leaned them against the side of his sound booth before disappearing out through the door again. She returned almost immediately, two large insulated delivery bags hanging from her shoulder. Another trip brought two more bags.

When she came back a fourth time, directing a dolly piled high with crates and equipment, Dawson picked up his pace. "Can I help you?"

Her eyes widened and her hands fisted as she stared at him for a few beats longer than seemed normal. Then she swallowed. "Oy. How long were you standing there?"

Huh. That was weird. Not many people could make casual sound so forced. "Not long. What are you doing here?"

"I, uh... food." She ran a hand through her chin-length blonde hair as she surveyed the mini-mountain she'd created with all her gear.

When no further words were forthcoming, Dawson walked around her to get to the sound booth. After studying the setup for a second, he flipped a few switches, and the lights came on at the back of the auditorium where they stood.

Her face was blank, and her eyes gave nothing away. "I'm with Heavenly Brew. We provide drinks and snacks during auditions and rehearsals."

"Heavenly Brew?"

"Best coffee shop in town, and we have a killer bakery, too. Well, not literally. That would be bad for business." If she was joking, her eyes didn't reflect it.

"Today's my first day. I'm not familiar with..."

She nodded before reaching for one of her tables, turning her back to him. "I know. Everyone knows. This is Gilead. Everything related to the passion play is town business. If someone has trouble remembering their lines, the whole town knows it. If the set makers run out of Perfectly Pink paint and end up using Salmon Pink for the sunset scene, we all hear about it. That only happened once, though. The hardware store stocks up on Perfectly Pink every December so we never have a sunset debacle again."

"Perfectly Pink?"

She clicked the legs on the second table into place before flipping it upright. "You wouldn't think Salmon Pink is all that different, but you've never heard such an uproar in all your life, I promise you."

Dawson's gaze moved from the tables to the woman, whose movements were efficient to the point of stark, to the two coffee urns she slipped into place on the end of one table. "Can I help you with anything?"

A shake of the head and still no eye contact. "Nah. I'm good. Besides, you've got plenty to do."

He looked back at the empty stage. "I do?"

Her movements stuttered for the barest second as she moved sugar and artificial sweetener from one of the crates to the table. "Did nobody tell you about auditions?"

"The guy from HR spent his morning convincing me I'm required to be here. If he was supposed to tell me any details about auditions, he didn't manage to work it into the conversation." Ugh. How did those words slip out? Hopefully he hadn't sounded too bitter.

"Why wouldn't you want to be here?"

"Easter isn't really my thing." And still, the words kept inexplicably falling out of his mouth. If he didn't know any better, he might think he actually wanted to talk about his issues with Easter.

"Not your thing?" She finally turned to him, her eyebrows nearly to her forehead. "Easter isn't really your thing?"

He forced a shrug. It was too late to take the words back.

"You're a believer. The college wouldn't have hired you otherwise."

"Yeah. I just don't like Easter."

Her eyebrows remained high on her forehead. "You took a job at Gilead Bible College, and you don't like Easter?"

He squinted. "What's the big deal?"

"Did you even look at the college's website before you took the job?"

He'd been a little busy with Christmas, family drama, and a desperate compulsion to find a job somewhere that he could be more useful than he felt in the secular world. "I don't remember."

"Did you look us up online *at all*?"

"Maybe?"

The woman who'd maybe sort of made a joke about a killer bakery without so much as a lip twitch or a sparkle in her eyes burst into laughter. "Sorry. Sorry. I'll stop..." Then she started laughing again.

And somehow, beyond all worldly reason, his anger faded like mist in the desert. He wasn't angry at the college. He wasn't angry at the HR guy who had made him feel trapped. And he wasn't angry at the woman who was clearly laughing at him, not with him. He didn't even understand exactly why she was laughing at him, but all he could do was grin as she wiped tears from her eyes.

She finally stood. "I'm sorry. That was rude. It's just..." Laughter bubbled up, and her eyes glowed with it, but she fought back and swallowed it down, once again returning to work and giving him her back. "It's just... this is Gilead Bible College. In Gilead, Kansas. You look either of those things up online, and the first thirty results you're given will be about the annual passion play. It's a big stinking deal around here, and not just in Gilead. It's a massive tourist draw. It pulls people in from all over the country."

He winced. Maybe he should have done a little more due diligence before taking the job. "It's that big?"

She gave him a quick glance, the laughter gone from her ice blue eyes. "It's not just a thing we do here in Gilead. It's woven into the fabric of our identity. It's who we are. 'Big' doesn't even begin to describe it. If Easter isn't your thing, then Gilead isn't your thing either."

2

L etty avoided staring at the college's new AV director. How on earth could he have taken a job in Gilead and not known about the annual passion play?

Unfathomable. That wasn't the only problem, though.

And he looked so lost. Granted, he also had a tall, dark, and handsome thing going on, but it didn't hide the struggle behind his cinnamon eyes.

She'd be lost, too, if she didn't like Easter. Easter was... everything. Her faith hinged on Easter. Paul talked about it in 1 Corinthians 15. Without the resurrection, the entirety of the Christian faith would fall apart.

This guy didn't seem to be against the resurrection, though. Just... the holiday?

Weird.

But not her problem.

Opening the first cooler, she began pulling out wrapped sandwiches and lining them up on one of the tables. Chicken salad, ham and cheese, turkey and bacon, and the vegan specialty of the day — jackfruit and avocado.

Before she opened the next insulated bag, she glanced at Dawson. "You're still here?"

He bit his bottom lip as he looked from her to the stage. "Do you know what I need to have set up for auditions?"

Oh, yeah. He didn't know. And she knew a little too well what being lost felt like. As much as she preferred to avoid new people, she couldn't very well walk away from him when she had the ability to help. "Well, um. I've never auditioned, but Heavenly Brew always provides the drinks and food, so I've been here a few times. They usually have around five different mics on stands around the stage plus cordless mics for the directorial team. Those folks usually sit somewhere around the fifth or sixth row, center stage. They need sound in the orchestra pit whenever they do the musical stuff, but that's not on the first night, so you should be okay for now."

He nodded and tapped something into his phone. "Anything else?"

"Mostly, just try not to make things squeal. Some of the people walk up to the mic and barely whisper, and some of them have huge booming voices. When the mics start squealing, it throws everyone off their game."

"As long as the other mics are muted, there shouldn't be a feedback loop."

She shrugged. "I don't know what a feedback loop is. I just know that everyone gets cranky when there's squealing. If you can make sure it doesn't happen, you'll be everyone's favorite new sound guy."

He walked off, mumbling to himself as he went. Then he stopped, turned around, and walked back to her. He held out his hand. "I'm Dawson. Sorry I didn't introduce myself sooner."

She stared at his hand for a minute before taking it. Great. They were going to end up BFFs at this rate despite all the anti-social vibes she normally threw off. "Letty. Nice to meet you."

As soon as she released his hand, he started for the front of the auditorium.

She watched him for an uncharacteristically long minute before shaking her head and returning to the insulated delivery bag in her hands. The pumpkin, banana, and lemon muffins weren't going to unload themselves.

"NEXT!"

Another thespian hopeful, this time on the far right microphone, spoke. "I'll be reading a dramatization of Judas Iscariot from John 12, the woman with the alabaster flask."

The director waved a hand, indicating he should continue.

"You fools! Why do we embrace what this woman did? She's nothing to us, and she cost us dearly. We should have sold the ointment. It was made from pure nard, for goodness sake. Do none of you get it? We're throwing money out like it's the rotten entrails left after the fish have been gutted. But where are we supposed to get our food? How are we supposed to meet our needs? You can be as foolish as you want, but I know the truth. Without funds, this entire operation falls apart."

Huh. That one was actually pretty good. Lots of passion... no pun intended.

The director's voice came over the house speakers. "Where did you find that piece?"

"I... uh... I wrote it."

"And why did you pick Judas?"

Even from this distance, Letty could see the color staining the boy's cheeks. "I... uh... I think people can relate to him more than we like to believe. We all battle selfishness in our hearts, even if we don't... uh... admit it."

"Thank you. We'll let you know. Next!" The director shouted

straight into the microphone, and Letty slapped her hands over her ears. The telltale squeal didn't come, though.

When she threw a glance Dawson's way, he winked at her.

"If he doesn't get the part, we need to get him on the writing team."

"Even if he gets the part, they'll want to poach him."

"Shh..."

Letty's gaze flew to the directors, who apparently hadn't realized one of them was holding a still-live mic.

The boy was still blushing as he made his way off stage, but he had a bounce in his step that hadn't been there before.

Dawson chuckled. "If something's going to be picked up on a mic, better that than a slam."

"Nah. The directors can be all business sometimes, but they're not mean-spirited."

He shook his head. "Is anybody in Gilead mean-spirited?"

"A few, but they're in the minority." Mrs. Alleghany came to mind, but she wouldn't be saying that out loud.

"I've met bossy, but I've yet to come across anyone who's outright mean."

A smile tugged at her lips. "Give it time. Now, want anything to eat or drink?"

"A can of soda would be nice, and maybe one of those sandwiches."

"Preference?"

He shook his head. "Surprise me."

NIGHT three of auditions was well under way as Letty stared at her dwindling supply of sandwiches. Had everyone picked Wednesday as the day to skip lunch?

Oh, well. She had enough muffins to make up for it.

Speaking of... She grabbed an apple spice muffin and tossed it to Dawson. He'd mentioned the night before that apple was his favorite pie. She'd made the muffins with him in mind. Not that he needed to know that.

Dawson snatched the muffin from the air, unwrapped it, took a whiff, and followed it up with a big bite. The broad smile he sent her said it all. She'd hit a home run with that one.

A woman Letty and all of Gilead knew well approached one of the mics. "I'll be doing a dramatization of Mary, the mother of Jesus."

"From when?" The director's voice was only slightly bored. Every female wanted to play Jesus' mother or Mary Magdalene. People rarely auditioned for the other female roles.

"The cross."

Another director picked up the conversation. "Proceed."

"My baby! My baby! Why? Why does he have to die? You did this!" She threw an accusing arm at the invisible passers-by that she was blaming. "You're killing the Savior of the world, the fruit of my womb..."

"Cut!" The director's voice put an end to the audition. "That's all we need. Thank you."

A quick side-eye showed her that the sound guy's eyebrows were at his hairline.

He looked over at her and blinked. "That was... intense."

She shrugged. "Overacting usually belongs to the freshmen."

"She didn't look much like a freshman."

"Nope. That's Mrs. Plugh. She keeps life in Gilead... lively."

"If all the auditions are like hers, I might be entertained enough to forget this is an Easter play."

She gave a little eyeroll. "Don't get your hopes up. Not every-one's as... energetic... as Mrs. Plugh."

His chuckle was low and easy. "You're here for all the auditions and rehearsals?"

She nodded. "The college pays me to be here. Or they pay for the food. I volunteer my time."

He dipped his chin toward the food table. "You make all that yourself?"

Was it wrong of her to want to tell him to mind his own business? Yes. Yes, it was wrong. She knew that. A lifetime of self-preservation, though, was hard to shake off, even within the warm confines of Gilead, Kansas. And there was something about the new AV guy. He unsettled her, but the reason was just out of her grasp.

Dawson's attention flitted back to the stage. An audition for Judas had just wrapped up, and another theater hopeful approached one of the mics. Dawson hit some buttons on his fancy sound board, and the new auditionee could be heard throughout the auditorium.

"I'll be reading the part of Jesus from Matthew, chapter twenty-seven, in King James. 'Eli, Eli, lama sabachthani?' Thank you."

One of the directors scratched his head. "That's it?"

The young man, who had been halfway to exit stage left, paused and turned. "Those are all of the Lord's words in Matthew 27."

"Pick a longer passage, then. Four words is not enough for us to know if you can act."

The young man winced. "Do you have any suggestions?"

"You're auditioning for the part of Jesus, and you don't know where else in Scripture he talks? Are you here on a dare?"

"I, uh... I mean... Uh... the Great Commission?"

"Sure. That'll work." The director's voice lacked enthusiasm.

The student fumbled with his phone as he tried to pull up the passage.

Dawson leaned Letty's way. "If he doesn't have the Great

Commission memorized, there's not a lot of hope of him getting a part, is there?"

"Not one with words."

"Please tell me he's not going to be dressed up like a camel."

She snorted. "Does this look like kindergarten? We use real animals here."

The widening of his eyes was evident, even in the auditorium's dim lighting. "You guys don't fool around, do you?"

"You're one of us now. *We* don't fool around. Like I told you, this play isn't a big deal. It's a huge deal. It's *the* deal in Gilead."

Dawson eyed her for a few beats before returning his attention to the stage with a grimace.

"So what's your deal with Easter? You've got to admit it's weird for a Christian not to like it."

He kept his eyes straight ahead. "I'm not sure I know you well enough to share that with you. Some things are private."

She could understand that. Better than most, even. She grabbed a brownie and walked it the three steps over to his booth. "Peace offering. I won't pry."

Dawson took in the food before sliding his gaze up to her eyes. He studied her for a moment before nodding. "Thank you."

As she turned back to her table, she caught a glimpse of who was heading toward a microphone on stage. "Be careful with this one. He's louder than a runaway tuba."

The corner of Dawson's mouth quirked up as he turned a knob and pulled a fader down. "Thanks for the warning."

3

If looks could kill, the microphone sitting on Dawson's desk would've turned to dust by now.

A knock at his door pulled his attention away from the offending piece of equipment. "Come in!"

Mr. Watersby, the head of HR, opened the door and stepped into Dawson's office.

After their last encounter, Dawson had looked the guy up and learned his name. He still wasn't sure what to think of someone who would offer up a backhanded threat to get him to do his job. At a minimum, though, this was a man whose name Dawson ought to know.

"I hear you're settling in well." The older man sank into a chair opposite Dawson.

"More or less."

"You didn't let that Belcher kid blast out everyone's eardrums at last night's auditions. No one's ever pulled that off before."

Belcher... ah. "Letty warned me when she saw him walking to the mic."

"Letty. Good girl. Quiet, observant. Most people don't notice her enough to listen to what she has to say."

Quiet? Were they talking about the same woman? The one who had laughed at him until she'd practically run out of oxygen, all because he didn't know that Gilead Bible College put on an annual Easter production? Not that he would change a moment of it. Having her there had been a good distraction from all that... Easteryness.

"What can I do for you today?"

Mr. Watersby offered a small smile. "Just wanted to make sure you don't plan on abandoning us any time soon."

Dawson sat back in his chair. "I'm a man of my word even when I don't realize I've given it."

The older man nodded before pushing himself back to his feet. "I hear there's a great coffee shop not too far from campus. You should go get yourself a cup if you're ever in the mood for a short walk."

The door closed silently behind the head of the HR Department. He'd sat in that chair for all of thirty seconds. Why had he even bothered?

With a shake of his head, Dawson cleared his thoughts. This town seemed to be filled with quirky characters. He'd gotten a pretty good sampling while sitting through audition after audition, but it was clear that the personality in Gilead didn't stop with those who paraded across the stage.

THE COWBELL CLANGED as Dawson opened the door. How... rustic.

Letty was chatting with a customer at the cash register. The older woman tapped her cane a couple of times on the floor before turning, coffee in hand. She gave Dawson a nod before calling over her shoulder, "You're not getting any younger, my dear."

The eyeroll Letty gave the woman's back said exactly how she felt about the parting comment. Then her eyes flitted to Dawson, and she smiled. A tight smile. Small. Forced. "What can I get you today?"

"What do you recommend?"

"One of everything." Her smile grew a tiny bit.

He'd take the win, even if he had no idea why seeing Letty smile felt like such a win. He'd barely met her. They hadn't exactly had any deep and meaningful conversations, either. He felt like he knew her, though. Weird. He was definitely being weird. "I'm not sure I can eat that much. Do you have anything with coconut?"

Her brow furrowed. "I can use coconut milk in almost any drink. The mocha with coconut milk is pretty good. I don't have anything coconut to eat today, but sometimes I have macaroons or coconut cream bars."

The walk from campus had been cold. January in Kansas was no joke. "I'll take the mocha with coconut milk, hot." His eyes scanned the menu. "And a turkey club, please. But what on earth is a coconut cream bar?"

"Think coconut cream pie, but in handheld form. They sell pretty quick whenever I have them."

"Hm. I'll have to keep my eye out for those." Dawson's heart felt lighter than it had in ages. Talking to Letty had done that. A silly simple conversation about coffee and food. What was it about this woman that made him feel so at home?

Letty rang up the order and gave him his total. He held his phone to the terminal to pay, trying to keep his wandering thoughts from showing on his face. Then he turned from the register and found himself a seat while he waited for his order. The shop was empty except for a woman with a toddler. The lull didn't fool him, though. The empty trays in the display case spoke to Heavenly Brew's brisk business.

He watched her as she worked on his order. She was effi-cient, graceful, and... familiar. Something about the way she moved rang some sort of bell in the back of his mind, echoing in his subconscious.

His gaze cut to the front window and the meager pedestrian traffic beyond. It didn't clear his mind the way he'd expected, though. With no soft reboot to be had, Dawson returned his attention to the woman behind the counter. The niggling feeling that he should know her from somewhere only intensified. It wasn't just that he felt comfortable around her. There was some-thing more to it. But what?

Love at first sight was bogus, as far as he was concerned, so this wasn't some fated-to-be-together romantic nonsense. He knew her from somewhere. The question was... where?

Letty brought his order to him, and he smiled his thanks. "Where are you from?"

Shadows slipped across her eyes before she frowned. "Gilead."

"Born and raised?"

"Might as well have been. There's nowhere else I call home. What about you? You know anyone in town besides me?"

Dawson almost grinned. "The head of HR at the college."

"Mr. Watersby? He's one of the best people this town has to offer."

If he was her idea of *good people*, then they might define that word differently. "I also ran into someone I know from Chicago. Preston Swift. I saw him at the grocery store. He's working on an endowment or something for the college."

His heart did a little skip-jump as Letty's smile washed over him. "Then he's working with Wendy. She handles fundraising stuff for the college. Your friend's in good hands if he's working with her."

He couldn't remember if Preston had introduced him to the

woman he'd been with or not. Seeing him had been a bit of a shock. Like seeing your high school math teacher at the beach. The image just didn't quite jive. Speaking of... Maybe she had family up north and they'd crossed paths somehow. That would explain why she seemed so familiar. "Ever been to Chicago?"

Her brows drew together. "Nope."

"What about San Francisco?" It was a long shot, but...

Steel shutters might as well have dropped over her face. Before he'd even finished the question, her expression transformed from cautious to locked down, Alcatraz style.

The cow bell sounded, and Letty walked away without another word or a backward glance.

Huh.

Odd.

He wasn't a ladies' man by any stretch of the imagination, but he was a decent conversationalist. Usually. At least, that's what he'd been led to believe.

Maybe if he'd told her she looked familiar? Or would that just make him seem creepy?

Yikes. Had their whole conversation been creepy? Had he even greeted her before asking where she was from?

He might need a refresher on the small talk skills Mom had forced him to learn.

Speaking of...

Dawson pulled out his phone. HEY MOM, OUT OF THE BLUE QUESTION. ARE THERE ANY FAMILIES BACK HOME WITH A GIRL NAMED LETTY WHO'S AROUND MY AGE OR MAYBE YOUNGER — LIKE 5 YEARS OR SO?

Her reply was almost instant. NOT THAT I CAN THINK OF. WHAT'S UP?

RAN INTO SOMEONE WHO SEEMS FAMILIAR, BUT I CAN'T QUITE PLACE IT.

MOST PEOPLE WOULD JUST ASK...

I TRIED THAT. DIDN'T GO OVER WELL.

PLEASE TELL ME YOU AT LEAST SAID HELLO OR REMARKED ON THE WEATHER BEFORE YOU GRILLED THE POOR THING.

Poor thing? That somehow implied helplessness. He'd only had a few interactions with her, but he'd become convinced that Letty was anything but helpless. She wasn't some frail, breakable damsel.

DAWSON?

OKAY, OKAY. I MIGHT NEED TO BRUSH UP ON MY SMALL TALK SKILLS.

AND YOU APOLOGIZED?

A smile pulled on his lips. His mom was a force to be reckoned with. Good thing she used that force for good. I'M ON IT.

Dawson finished off his sandwich while watching the endless stream of customers come and go. His back corner table provided a clear view of everyone, but nobody seemed to notice him.

Not a single person came in simply to order a drink and leave. Everybody had something to say, and Letty listened to and spoke with each person. Her gaze occasionally shot to him, and if he wasn't mistaken, she sported a blush a couple of different times. The time she took with each customer, though, was something special. Aside from the eyeroll he'd witnessed when he'd first gotten to the shop, Letty showed interest in each person and whatever they told her.

Hm. What had Mr. Watersby said about her? Quiet, observant, not noticed.

The quiet and observant part was obvious. She was a listener. She responded when spoken to, but she rarely volunteered much. Not noticed, though? Dawson was half-convinced that the people who came into the shop came to see Letty more than they came in to get coffee or food. The question was, did people really see her? Or did they just see who they thought she was? Or who they wanted her to be?

As soon as there was a break in customers, Dawson cleared his table and made his way to the register. Letty was busy wiping down the counter by the espresso maker, but he didn't let that deter him. "I'm sorry about earlier."

She didn't bother to lift her eyes from her task. "No problem."

"You seem familiar, and I wondered if our paths have crossed before. I didn't mean to make you uncomfortable."

Her gaze met his for a millisecond before returning to her task. It was long enough, though, for him to see that the shutters were still in place. Maybe even padlocked. "I doubt we've met. I just have one of those faces. And I live an entirely uneventful life here in Gilead."

Except it wasn't so much the face that made her seem familiar. It was the way she moved. Her laugh, even. She could deny it all she wanted, but he'd only ever felt this connected to someone once before, and that had been... different.

Dawson shut the thought down before his mind could wander too far down that path. "Well, I'll see you tonight."

"Tonight?"

"At auditions."

Her eyes slid closed for a few beats before opening again, but she didn't bother raising her gaze from the coffee stain that had long since been wiped clean. "Right. I'm not sure I'll be there. I hope auditions go well, though."

4

Letty stared at Dawson's retreating back.

She'd never been so thankful to have her coffee shop completely to herself. It would probably only last for two breaths, but she would savor those breaths nonetheless.

San Francisco.

Terror skidded through her chest like old tires on wet asphalt. The mere thought of that city nearly brought her to her knees.

So much for having moved on.

She'd been in Gilead for over a decade, and in that time, she'd changed everything she could about who she was. She'd reinvented herself, and she'd finally made peace with this life and with who she'd become.

An old lesson from high school physics came to mind. Because that was normal. Two objects couldn't exist in the same space at the same time. Her past couldn't collide with her present, not without serious collateral damage. And that collateral damage? It would be her.

Her life. Her peace. Her joy. Her world.

She grabbed her phone before she could change her mind. CAN YOU COVER AUDITIONS FOR ME? SOMETHING'S COME UP.

Philip's reply came a few minutes later. ANYTHING I NEED TO WORRY ABOUT?

She bit her bottom lip. Philip knew her better than anyone in Gilead. He still didn't know about this, though. And she wasn't sure she was ready to tell him. NOPE. JUST OVERBOOKED MYSELF. IT'S HARD TO GET UP AT 3AM TO BAKE WHEN I'M AT AUDITIONS UNTIL 10PM.

PRETTY SURE I WARNED YOU ABOUT THAT.

HUSH, OLD MAN. NOBODY LIKES A KNOW-IT-ALL.

He fired back a GIF of an octogenarian hunched over a walker.

When nothing further came through, she tucked her phone into her back pocket. He'd do it. Silence was as good as consent with Philip. He wasn't exactly a big talker, one of the things she liked most about him.

THE SUN HAD SET, and Letty was stretched out on the couch, her feet on the coffee table. She should be doing something productive, but tomorrow would come soon enough. Then she'd be busy all day long. An evening of sloth wasn't the end of the world.

And yet she could barely make herself stay put. If she didn't do something soon, she might just burst out of her own skin.

Her phone dinged with an incoming text.

THE SOUND GUY ASKED ABOUT YOU. WAS HE HITTING ON YOU? IS THAT WHY YOU DIDN'T WANT TO BE HERE?

Letty sighed at the text. So much for Philip being a man of few words. NO HITTING INVOLVED. JUST TIRED.

He seems nice enough. Are you sure he didn't scare you away?

No way was she giving him a real answer. Have you ever known me to be scared?

Yes. That's what concerns me.

Of course he'd go there. She didn't scare easily, but when they'd first met, she'd jumped a foot in the air at every single sound she hadn't seen coming. Don't worry, Old Man. I just don't want to mess up the morning recipes because I'm too tired to see straight.

The next morning started pretty much like any other. The stream of customers was never-ending, and each person had an opinion they felt compelled to share.

Mrs. Alleghany stood there, a gleam in her eyes. "Did you hear about the new young man working at the college? He does technical stuff. Quite a handsome fellow, too, from what I hear. Savannah Smith's niece saw him at auditions last night and told her aunt all about it."

Letty tried to bite back her grimace. "Um... did you want any coffee today?"

The steel-haired woman harrumphed. "Is that all you think about?"

Letty glanced over at the kitchen door. She could go for an escape right about now. Then she took in the still-growing line and sighed. "We're a coffee shop. It's sort of my job to think about coffee."

Mrs. Alleghany gave a long-suffering sigh. "Fine. One hot coffee to go. You're starting to get a little long in the tooth, you know. If he's working at the Bible college, I'm sure he's a fine

Christian man. You should bake him a pie to welcome him to town."

"Yeah, and show a little cleavage when you deliver it!" The voice came from near the door, but the speaker was hidden by the line.

Letty grabbed the coffee Cici held out to her and handed it to the town's biggest gossip. "On the house, Mrs. Alleghany. Have a nice day. Next!"

Cici, the high school girl who helped during the early morning rush, stood there with her shoulders shaking. "I'm not laughing. I promise. And cleavage or not, you don't look a day over fifty."

Letty snorted. She was still shy of thirty, and they all knew it.

The next customer was at the register. "Don't listen to her, Letty, dear. You're a spring chicken. Are you even old enough to drink?"

With a shake of her head, she turned to the gentleman who always wore slacks and a button-up shirt, whether he was spending his day gardening or socializing. "Good morning, Mr. Abrams. How's the arthritis this morning?"

"A storm's coming. I can feel it in my bones."

Nobody laughed. Mr. Abrams' bones hadn't been wrong yet.

"Want the usual?"

"You know it, sweetheart. So... how old are you, anyway? Probably too young for a crotchety old man like me..."

Letty took the hot mocha from Cici and handed it to one of her favorite town residents. "Well, Mr. Abrams, I'm old enough to drink but not so old that I'm ready to shop for a cemetery plot."

"How long's it been since you went on a date, dear? I seem to recall..."

"It's on the house. I can help the next person!"

Sally stopped laughing long enough to order. "I need two

vanilla lattes, one caramel macchiato, and an Americano with an extra shot."

"You got it." Letty wrote the orders on the cups and passed them off to Cici.

"If I ask about your love life, will my order be on the house, too?"

"Ha. You wish. If you ask about my love life, I'll ask about yours."

Sally held her hands up in surrender. "You fight dirty, Letty Stanton."

"And don't you forget it." She winked at her friend before turning to the next customer.

"Good morning, dear. Can I get one of your almond croissants, please? And a cup of cinnamon spice tea, please."

"Of course, Mrs. Butler. Coming right up."

As Letty handed over the plated pastry, the soft-spoken woman dropped her voice to a whisper. "The college's new AV guy is going to run lights and sound for the play. Maybe you'll get a chance to meet him at auditions..."

SHE'D ONLY MANAGED to avoid auditions for one night. It didn't really count as a good run, but regardless — her reprieve had ended. Philip had bailed on her for this last night of auditions.. He'd told her to woman-up and do her job. Such a charmer, that one.

Friday night saw Letty hauling sandwiches and pastries into the back of the auditorium. During the actual passion play, people could buy food at the concession stand. For auditions and rehearsal, though? Nobody wanted the bother of having to clean up an additional space. It was easier to set up on tables at the back of the auditorium. The only problem came when the auditorium got used for something else and she had to break all her tables back down. She was used to it, though. And Heavenly Brew got some great promo out of it, so there was that.

"Long time no see." Dawson's voice reverberated throughout the auditorium, coming from everywhere at once, so it took her a moment to find him in the hidden recesses of the stage.

"Isn't using the mic like that an abuse of power?"

His snort echoed around her before he left the mic and hopped off the stage to approach her. "Need any help?"

"Nah. I got it." Hopefully he wouldn't bring up her weirdness from earlier in the week.

He watched her without speaking. Only a minute or two passed before he turned away and walked over to the nearby open-walled space that housed the sound and light boards. "I enjoyed getting to know Philip. Gilead's full of interesting people."

It was her turn to snort. "Interesting? You don't know the half of it."

His gaze lingered on her before moving back to his equipment, where he started sliding faders up and bringing the stage lights on.

Letty released a silent sigh.

She liked Dawson. She wasn't even sure what it was about him, but she liked him. He made her want to smile.

Except for when he'd brought up San Francisco.

5

Dawson followed Letty's movements out of the corner of his eye. Not that he had planned to spend his time staring at her. He couldn't help it, though. His eyes kept finding their way over to her, and there didn't seem to be much he could do about it.

Her movements were efficient as people began streaming into the auditorium and mobbing her table. Whatever hesitation people'd had that first night of auditions had evaporated. Her table was swarmed before Dawson could so much as scratch the back of his neck.

One of the weird things about Gilead? Everybody and their brother came out to watch the auditions. The first night had apparently been slow-going compared to the full-on peopling assault the rest of the auditions had turned into. It wasn't just the food table they were interested in, either. Every night, at least a dozen people approached his sound booth and struck up random conversations.

Small towns were so... bizarre.

People eventually drifted away from Letty's table, their cups and plates full. They stood in little groupings in the back of the auditorium — the only place food and drink other than bottled water was allowed.

As those little groupings meandered farther away, Dawson tossed a glance at Letty. He had a question that had been burning to get out, but he hadn't dared voice it the last few nights. Philip hadn't exactly struck him as a willing font of information. "Why is everyone so friendly?"

Letty's chuckle made his heart smile. "What makes you think they're friendly?"

"Complete strangers stop by this booth every single night to ask how my parents are doing, if I've found a local church yet, and how long I've been in the AV business. They're all so interested in my life that it's kind of..."

"Disconcerting?"

"I was going to say 'annoying,' but I was afraid it would sound rude."

"Oh, it totally sounds rude. When you've lived here for a while, though, you'll begin to realize that sometimes a touch of rudeness is the only way to be heard above all the noise."

Dawson shook his head before adjusting the volume for a pimple-faced youth who didn't look old enough for his voice to have changed yet. "Having so many people interested in my well-being is going to take some getting used to."

Letty hummed a low sound.

It was the sound she made when she wanted to laugh but was trying to be quiet. Strange as it seemed, he'd missed that sound the last few nights. And how weird was it that he'd barely met her and yet already knew what that sound meant?

"Most folks around here are genuinely caring," she said. "They're also mining you for information, though. Everybody wants to know what they can about the new AV guy at the college, but if I was going to put money on it, I'd say at least a few of them were trying to figure out if they could set you up with their daughters, nieces, or granddaughters."

A stone dropped in Dawson's stomach while his panic took flight. Such weird conflicting feelings. "You're kidding, right?"

Softness entered Letty's aquamarine eyes, tempting him with her sympathy. "We have a small local dating pool. Most folks in town don't mind if a loved one dates a college student, but they'd much rather they date someone who's setting down roots in town. Less likelihood of their kiddo moving across country come graduation time."

"So all the friendliness is actually scheming?"

Letty gave a shrug. "Some of it's scheming, yeah. But just because there's scheming involved doesn't mean they're not also friendly."

Dawson's attention went back to the stage as a young man who could have easily been a linebacker lumbered toward one of the microphones.

DAWSON'S first full Saturday in Gilead started with a leaky faucet in his rental home. That the hardware store didn't open until 11am had to be criminal, too. With that thought, he opened the door to Heavenly Brew and inhaled deeply of the coffee and sweet pastry-scented air.

The line to the register stood five deep, so he stepped up to it, planning to wait his turn.

As time passed, though, he realized the line was inching along slower than normal. The dining room was wrecked, too. It looked like Letty was on her own during the weekend morning rush.

He should just wait his turn, get his morning coffee, and

leave like a normal person. He couldn't quite make himself do that, though.

A grey tub with dishes in it sat on the kitchen side of the counter like a child put into time-out and then forgotten. With a snap decision, Dawson stepped out of line, walked over to the tub, and walked it into the kitchen. He unloaded the dishes by the three-sink washing station, grabbed himself a clean towel and the spray bottle labeled FOR TABLES ONLY, and headed back into the dining area.

In short order, he'd cleared the dishes from all the tables and gotten them wiped down. Returning to the kitchen, it only took him a minute to figure out which of the sinks was for washing, and he got to work. A high school summer stint in the fast-food industry had taught him the three-sink method. Wash, rinse, sanitize.

He broke his dishwashing up with three more trips to the dining room to collect dishes and wipe down tables. Finally, on his last trip out there, it seemed like things had started to slow down. How Letty did this on a regular basis was anybody's guess. She needed at least two more full-time employees, from what he could see.

As Dawson placed the last of the dishes onto the drying rack, the kitchen door swung open. Letty stood there, hand on her hip. Did she want to thank him or tell him to mind his own business next time? Her look gave nothing away.

She finally let out a breath and gave him a nod. "Breakfast's on the house if you want something."

If he wanted something? He could probably eat everything left in her display case if she gave him half a chance. "I could maybe go for something."

∾

LETTY SAT down across from him, a sensible egg and avocado wrap on her plate. Dawson, on the other hand, had a ham and egg breakfast sandwich, an almond croissant, and two bananas on his plate. And he figured he'd still be walking away hungry.

"Don't you normally have someone in here helping you?"

She bit off half her wrap in a single go. "Mm-hm. Shcldnsk."

Dawson lifted an eyebrow. "I caught the first part. You know, the mm-hm part."

Color stained Letty's cheeks as she swallowed. "She called in sick."

"And you don't have backup staff?"

"Philip helps me if I get in a pinch, but he's out of town and won't be back 'til afternoon."

"Ah. That explains why you were at auditions last night."

She took another bite, smaller this time.

"You had a high school girl in here sometime this last week. Right? Or did I imagine that?"

"Cici. She and one of her sisters are in here Monday through Friday. Weekend help is harder to find."

"How come? I'd expect you'd have more high school students who want to work weekends than weekdays. And how can they work during the week if they have school, anyway? Are they working for school credit or something?"

Letty polished off the rest of her wrap. "Cici and her sisters are homeschooled. They work here to save up money for college, and because their folks are flexible with their school schedule, they can be here to help with breakfast and lunch rushes. It's a win-win."

"And weekends?"

"Weekends are hard. Cici and her sisters are an anomaly. A blessing, but an anomaly. Most high school and college students think they want a weekend job until they realize they need to be here by six in the morning and that they'll mostly be on their feet all day."

Dawson, his plate now clean, too, reached for his mocha with coconut milk. "Do you need a weekend person to run the register or make the drinks?"

"Both would be ideal. Weekends are busy, though, so even if all they do is keep the dining room clean, stock the display case, and pitch in with dishes, I'd be better off than I am now."

"I know a thing or two about working with college students. This might be my first stint at a Christian institution, but I've been working in higher education for a while now. Any help I'm allowed to hire is always college students. Work study and all that. Sometimes I need to have three or four hiring events during the year just to replace all the people who decided it was okay to stop showing up to work without a word of warning. There are always some gems in the bunch, but they're the minority."

The cowbell on the front door clanged. Letty's back was to the door, but it didn't matter. Dawson felt her sigh all the way to his bones as she slowly rose from her seat and turned to greet the new customer.

Maybe someone involved in the play might want to pick up a few hours on the weekend. He'd have to keep an ear to the ground and see if anyone needed work. Surely someone out there thought six in the morning on a Saturday was an ideal start time for a job.

Well... at least an acceptable start time. Or tolerable. Tolerable would work.

6

L etty tried to glare at Dawson. "You should leave."

He ignored her and carried another tub of dirty dishes to the kitchen.

When he came out fifteen minutes later carrying a tray of cookies for the display case, she gave up on the glare. It would be rude to glare at him when he was working so hard. Instead, she slid open the glass door and removed the empty tray for him.

He reached out to take the empty tray from her, but his gaze snagged on the line of people waiting to order. It had grown from three to seven in the time it had taken him to slide the cookies into place.

He tipped his chin toward the waiting customers. "Show me how to enter an order, and I'll take over the register so you can actually make the drinks."

Letty could have kissed him. On the cheek. Briefly. If there weren't so many witnesses.

Shaking her head at her own crazy thoughts, she stepped over to the register and showed him how to enter an order. "If they have substitutions or want anything fancy, just write it on the cup for me. Don't worry about updating their order in the register. You know, if they want soy milk or something like that."

Dawson gave her an absent nod, his eyes focused on the register, as she slipped away to start on the backlog of drinks she needed to make.

Several minutes passed as Dawson continued to take orders, dish up pastries for people, and slide empty cups into the lineup for her to work on. He'd even figured out the basics of sandwich-making as she'd called instructions to him so he could make a turkey club for one of the customers.

It all came to a screeching halt, though, when Letty picked up a cup and read the drink instructions. The entire side of the cup was covered in the half-legible scribbles of a permanent marker.

Chai Latte
Dirty
Almond Milk
Extra Whip
Your Phone #
So Customer Can Call You
For a Date

Letty's attention was stuck on the last three lines, but she fought for control so she wouldn't show her reaction. "What's *Dirty*?"

"That's what caught your eye?" Dawson lifted an eyebrow as he glanced her way.

She kept her eyes down. If she made eye contact, she'd go up in flames. She rarely blushed, but when she did, she lit up like Rockefeller Center at Christmas. It wasn't a good look on her.

"It means extra chai."

She turned back to her workstation. "We just say extra chai."

Dawson snorted as he turned back to the register.

"Who's this for, anyway?"

The corner of his mouth tipped up, and his eyes shone with repressed laughter. "How many people normally hit you up for your number? Is it such a regular occurrence that you can't figure out which of the eligible men here it might be?"

Was there a good way to answer? No. No, there was not.

For the first couple of years after she'd settled in Gilead, guys had tried to ask her out. She'd shut them all down pretty hard — and not always politely.

Philip had eventually put the word out that people needed to leave her alone. Even the interfering mamas and aunties had stopped sniffing around and telling her about the "sweet young man" in their lives. Thankfully.

After that, she'd kind of become part of the furniture. She was just there. Everyone got so used to her presence that they didn't really see her anymore. They knew where she was when they needed something from her — like a great cup of coffee. Other than that, though, she was pretty much invisible.

Exactly how she liked it. Mostly. Invisibility could get lonely sometimes.

"Chai latte with almond milk, extra chai!" Letty called the order out as she placed it on the pick-up counter.

Dawson reached one of his long arms over, snagged the cup, and took a drink. He gave her a wink before turning back to the waiting customers.

She should have known.

Dawson showing up in town had stirred everything up. Everyone, too. The crazy thing was, nobody cornered her to talk about their son, nephew, grandson, or new stepbrother who she should consider dating. Instead, every single person in the town of Gilead seemed determined that she somehow end up with Dawson. How the times had changed.

Now he was throwing his weight behind that nonsense, too?

She'd fire him if she wasn't so desperate for the help. And if he was actually her employee. Minor details.

LETTY FLIPPED the switch to turn off the neon sign in the front window. They were officially closed, and not a minute too soon. She was ready to drop on her feet.

"Is the idea of going on a date with me so abhorrent?"

She gave Dawson some side-eye before rubbing a hand down her face. "Seriously? That's the thing you want to talk about right now?"

His laugh filled the dining area with light.

Letty felt like a scorpion who wanted to scurry back into a corner where it was dark. Better a scorpion than a cockroach, right?

"I'm just giving you a hard time."

"It's not you. It's..."

"You?"

A smile tugged at the corner of her mouth. "Something like that."

He stepped into her space, and she resisted the urge to back up. He wasn't unreasonably close. Her personal bubble was bigger than most, and not everyone recognized that.

Dawson tipped his head until he caught her eye. "I'm sorry if I stepped out of line. You were working so hard, and I just wanted to make you laugh. I didn't mean to make you uncomfortable. For all I know, you're madly in love with someone."

"So... you weren't asking me out?" Was that disappointment swirling around and getting all tangled up in her middle?

He gave her a broad smile. "I was... testing the waters? To see if my asking you out would be welcome. I get the feeling it wouldn't be, and I can accept that. We're going to be spending a lot of time together, and I'd like us to be friends. I don't want to cross any line that'll make you want to avoid me."

Wow. That was a full-on complete answer. Who knew a guy could do that? "Philip usually just grunts when I ask him a question. You use way more words than I'm used to."

His eyes softened before he turned away to start wiping down the tables. "Who's Philip, anyway? I mean, I met him and all. But who is he to you?"

This guy was developing a habit of asking her all the hard questions. "He took me in when I arrived in Gilead."

"Family?"

"Nah. Not really. I, uh... I was sleeping at the bus depot. I'd run out of money, I guess. Something woke me up, and when I opened my eyes, Philip was squatting down at eye level in front of me. He held out a cup of hot coffee and a pastry bag that said Heavenly Brew on it. He offered me a place to stay while I got myself sorted out. And here I am."

Dawson's eyes widened, and Letty took an instinctive step back. She'd said too much. Way more than she normally said, and definitely too much for this kind-hearted man to handle.

"How old were you?"

She shrugged. "Doesn't matter. It was a long time ago."

His eyes swept over the dining room before settling back on her. A muscle ticked in his jaw. "Tell me what needs to be done."

Letty stuffed her hands into her pockets. "What do you mean?"

"To close up. Wipe down the tables? Put the chairs up? Give me some marching orders, and I'll get started."

"You don't have to stay. I can do it."

He ran a hand down his face, jaw still tight. "I'm not leaving you here to do it all alone. If we work together, we'll knock everything out in no time. Just tell me what comes first."

What was his problem? He needed to leave so she could pick

up the tattered remnants of her cloak of invisibility and pull it back around her shoulders. Dawson did things to her. He made her stomach pinch and roll. It was like she was on the edge of a cliff staring into the brightness of the Pacific Ocean. The thought of falling forward into the warm embrace of the air as the frigid water rushed to meet her was as exhilarating as it was terrifying.

Self-preservation won out. She wouldn't be jumping into any warm embraces today, imaginary or otherwise. Getting rid of this guy wouldn't be so easy, though. "Wipe the tables and chairs with the sanitizing cleaner. When they're dry, flip the chairs onto the tables. Then sweep and mop. I'll work on the kitchen and bathroom."

He gave a single nod before heading toward the shelf where he'd been storing the table cleaner between uses.

7

Dawson's teeth were clenched as he wiped down the last of the tables.

He didn't know which made him angrier — that Letty had been alone and vulnerable and sleeping in a bus station or that she'd accepted food and shelter from a complete stranger twenty or thirty years her senior... and that the man in question may well have had vile intentions.

He pulled in a deep breath through his nose, bowed his head, and called out to the God who had all the answers. *What happened to her? How can I get her to open up? Is it even any of my business? Why do I care so much? Help me. Help me to know... Help me to know Your will and to walk in it here...*

The swinging of the kitchen door pulled him from the thoughts he was only marginally managing to articulate into prayer.

"Ready to sweep?" Letty's face was open, but her eyes were guarded.

He hadn't missed the way she'd stepped away from him earlier. He usually managed to keep a rein on his emotions. He'd been told more than once that he had a great poker face. That mask had failed him, though, when she'd told him how she came to be in Gilead, and he needed to try to repair the damage he'd done.

"Yeah. Everything's wiped. I just need to put up the chairs that've dried."

She nodded. "You do that, and I'll start behind you with the sweeping."

They worked in silence, completing the sweeping and then the mopping. When everything was done and the cleaning supplies had all been tucked away where they belonged, Letty glanced from him to the front door.

"Um... thank you? For the help, I mean. Thank you."

Yeah... subtlety had never been his strong suit. "I have to ask. Philip found you at the bus depot and took you home?"

"Yeah." One word, no eye contact. Guilt? Shame? Fear? This woman was going to drive him to madness with all the little walls she'd built around herself.

"To live with him?" Philip hadn't been overtly creepy when they'd met at auditions, but if she'd been in Gilead a decade, she couldn't have been much more than sixteen or seventeen when she'd met Philip. The thought made Dawson's stomach heave.

She snorted. "I'm not the most trusting individual. So, no. He let me crash in the apartment above the coffee shop. It was mostly just a cobweb-filled storage space back then. It was outfitted with a small kitchenette and bathroom, but it wasn't furnished or anything. He let me earn my keep by cleaning it out and going through all the junk he'd piled up there over the years."

Relief flooded his veins. He hadn't even realized how high his tense shoulders had climbed until they dropped on his next exhale. Still... "How old were you?"

Those familiar shutters dropped down over her eyes. "Old enough."

He'd known better than to get too personal, but he hadn't been able to help himself. The thought of someone taking advantage of her when she was vulnerable like that... She didn't want to know that the mere thought of it made his lunch threaten to reappear. So he offered a nod. "Fair enough. You were safe, though?"

"With Philip? Always."

He shouldn't read more into her answer than she was saying. The implication was there, though, and he couldn't ignore it. Philip hadn't been a threat to her. But before Philip? She hadn't been safe. Wherever she'd come from had not been a safe place.

The other implication, of course, was that her past before she landed in Gilead was off-limits. He could live with that. For now. He'd already gotten more from her than he'd expected.

He sighed and injected more calm into his voice than he felt. "Good. Everyone should have a safe place to land when life knocks them sideways."

DAWSON COULDN'T LEAVE WELL ENOUGH ALONE. He was hardwired to tug at every single thread until the entire blanket came unraveled.

Or, in this case, until the secrets came into the light.

Only Letty's life wasn't a blanket, and if he tugged too hard, she might be the thing that came unraveled, and he didn't want that.

What was it about that woman that made him want to see all the way into her soul?

He was going to tread with care. He was going to tread with care. He was going to tread with care.

He'd repeated the mantra to himself more than once since he'd left Heavenly Brew the night before.

Nonetheless, he arrived at church bright and early. He'd participated in enough idle chitchat while running the register yesterday to know exactly where Letty attended church. He even knew which Sunday school class was hers.

Normally, he would avoid Sunday school like the plague until he was sure about the church. Going to Sunday school meant people would ask for your name and phone number. It meant you were connected. Personally, he preferred not to be connected until he knew the church wasn't teaching something wackadoo. Desperate times and all that, though.

He knew Letty from somewhere. He grew more sure of it with each passing interaction, each conversation, each glance. It had to be from before she'd landed in Gilead, though. Nothing else made sense.

Which meant he'd known her when her life had not been safe. Whatever had gone on, he hadn't known about it. He hadn't seen. He hadn't been aware. And because of that, he hadn't made any attempt to protect or help her.

His late fiancée had always told him he had a hero complex. But he didn't. Not really. He just... He couldn't stand the thought that someone had been hurting, and he'd been blind to it. Or worse, that someone had been in peril and he'd done nothing.

Whatever trouble hid in Letty's past, it had to have been in her childhood. Her age — which he was admittedly still guessing at — and her decade in Gilead meant she'd been a kid or close to it whenever the *not safe* part of her past had occurred.

"Good morning! Welcome to Fount of Grace Community Church."

Dawson had known the name before he came, but hearing someone say it was... "That's quite a mouthful."

The man who'd greeted him shrugged. "Every few years someone makes a motion to change it to Gilead Community Church, but since one of the meanings of *Gilead* is 'perpetual fountain,' we always end up back where we started. What a better fountain to have than one of grace?"

That was a lot of information. "Um... sure."

The guy laughed. "Sorry. You didn't actually want to know any of that, did you? Sometimes my mouth runs away with me. I'm Thomas Malone, the pastor here at Fount of Grace."

He took the proffered hand. "Dawson Bauer."

"Nice to meet you, Dawson. Can I help you find a class this morning?"

"Um..." He'd kind of just planned on staking the place out and following Letty to her class when she arrived.

"We have a great Sunday school class that most of our young singles attend." The pastor looked at him, eyebrows lifted.

"Like, a college class?" He might still be single, but in church Sunday school terms, he wasn't exactly young.

"Oh, no, no. Sorry. Should have been more clear. This class isn't specifically for singles or young people or anything. It's just the one that most of our twenty-something and thirty-something singles gravitate toward."

"Umm." He fully intended on ending up in Letty's class even if it meant he had to walk out of whatever class the pastor herded him into.

"Letty's in the class. I believe you know her?"

The man was a mind reader. Or very discerning. Then again, maybe he just knew everyone and everything the way people in Gilead seemed to. "Sure. I'll give it a try."

Laughter danced in the pastor's eyes for a few seconds before he headed toward a hallway. "Follow me."

Twenty minutes and two cups of flavorless coffee later, people finally began filtering into the classroom.

The chairs were arranged at narrow, long tables that all faced the front of the room. It had a little more of a classroom feel than Dawson was used to in Sunday school, but as people came through the door and began filling the tables, it became apparent that the arrangement was more about space than anything else. It did nothing to stifle people's conversations or prevent them from turning around and chatting with those around them.

Another ten minutes — just as the teacher was stepping up to the front of the class — and Letty came rushing through the door. She was more flustered than Dawson had seen her. Not that he knew her all that well, but based on how she'd talked about her employees, he didn't think Letty was the type to be comfortable showing up late. The blush staining her cheeks seemed to confirm his thoughts.

She mouthed *sorry* to the teacher before taking the only remaining open seat in the class.

It probably wasn't an accident that Letty ended up in the seat next to his.

Someone had almost sat in that seat more than once, only for another person in the class to clear their throat loudly. He might have heard "Don't sit there" threaded through somebody's fake cough at one point, too.

He didn't know whether to laugh at these people or thank them. For now, he'd do the smart thing.

He gave Letty a nod and a smile, then turned his attention to the teacher and did his best to avoid staring at the intriguing woman next to him.

8

Letty sat in the back pew. Not that she supported designated pews or anything like that, but everybody in town knew the back pew over on the far right was hers. She liked to be where she could see everyone and still kind of keep an eye on the door.

Old habits and all that.

The pew shifted as someone sat a few feet down from her. She couldn't seem to escape this guy. "I'm going to start thinking you're following me if you're not careful."

Dawson's eyebrows shot up. "Is that a problem?"

She shrugged. "Depends on why, I guess."

His eyes lit with his smile. "If it helps, I started out on the far left, fifth row from the back."

She glanced that way. Ah. Mrs. Elden's grandchildren were visiting. "The ten-year-old sings like an angel. You might actually want to sit over there."

He gave her side-eye and pointed at his pants. "Yeah, but the three-year-old bathed himself in maple syrup this morning and then acted like I was his favorite climbing tree."

"Ooh. Yeah, I see your dilemma." The munchkin had

managed to sticky-ify Dawson's pants, shirt, and... um... yep... his hair, too. Should she tell him his hair looked like he'd gelled a swath of it into place? He probably already knew...

"You like this church?"

She nodded. "It's good. Solid teaching. Not much in the way of fanfare, but I don't need a sales pitch with my sermon, so I like it."

The man beside her chuckled. "I visited a friend's church a few years back. They had a light show when the pastor came out. A legit light show. With smoke machine and everything."

"You're a lights guy, though. I'd think you'd go for that kind of thing."

His eyes widened. "If the lighting guy is doing his job, you don't even know he's there. Same with sound. They're supposed to have a subtle touch. You know, draw attention where it needs to be, highlight certain things without people realizing they're being highlighted. He's not supposed to be a big enough part of the performance to get noticed."

"A sermon's different than a performance, though."

"Not at that church, it wasn't. But I agree, it should be. A church service should draw attention to the Word, not to the people conducting the service."

Humble. He had to be. He wouldn't be able to do his job the way he described otherwise.

"Letty-lou!" Audrey didn't know how to talk at anything other than full volume. She could get away with it because she was four years old and adorable as all get-out. "I haven' seen you in fo'ever! I missed you!"

Letty hugged the girl. "Hey there, Audrey-boo. How was Sunday school?"

"I only got in t'ouble for talking twice! I did ext'a good!"

"Only twice? That's amazing! You're doing so much better. I'm proud of you."

"Being quiet is ha'd. I have so many things I wanna say."

Letty tugged on one of the girl's braids. "Imagine how much fun you'll have when you learn to write. You'll be able to write down all your fun stories and keep them so you can share them when it's okay to talk."

"I can w'ite." Audrey's pout made her look like the darling she was.

"Tell me about what you wrote this week."

Audrey's eyes slid from Letty's face to the man sitting a bit down the pew from her. An unusual bout of shyness hit the girl, and she tucked herself into Letty's arms and whisper-shouted close to her ear. "I w'ote my name."

Letty let the girl burrow. "Ah. That's an important thing to write. You'll use that for the rest of your life. So did you learn to write Audrey or Audrey-boo?"

Letty had landed in Gilead under dubious circumstances, but little girl giggles warm against her neck were enough to remind her of all the reasons she'd stayed.

LETTY WAS STILL TUCKING her Bible into her bag — she really needed to clean that thing out — when she felt a presence at her back.

"You're joining us for lunch, right?" Sally's words were the kind of no-nonsense crisp that's forceful and warm all at the same time.

"Depends. What's on the menu?"

Sally smacked her on the arm.

"Mommy! No hitting." Audrey gave her mom a fierce frown, hands on her hips.

"Oops. My mistake. I thought I saw a spider on her arm."

Letty rolled her eyes.

"You should join us, Dawson." Sally's order — uh... invitation? — left little room for argument.

Dawson's eyebrows climbed his forehead. "I... mhm..."

"I promise not to hit you. Probably."

Audrey's infectious grin lit up her little girl face, her shyness from earlier long gone. "I'll make shuh she behaves. Sometimes mommies need help wi' that."

When Letty finally got around to looking at the man in question, she found his eyes on her rather than on the invitation-wielding mother-daughter duo.

"I don't want to intrude."

She chewed her bottom lip for a few seconds longer than polite before giving the new man in town a nod. "If you think you're intruding, you haven't gotten to know your new town very well yet. Or its people."

He hid his wince, mostly.

Letty had years of practice studying facial expressions to anticipate a person's mood and actions. She wouldn't have caught the pinching around his eyes otherwise.

Dawson returned her nod before looking to Sally. "I'd love to join you. Thank you for the invitation."

Not that lunch with Sally and Audrey was ever quiet or boring, but today's lunch just got a whole lot more interesting.

"Sit he'e!" The chair's legs gave a screech against the scuffed wood floor as Audrey pulled it out for Dawson.

He sank gingerly into his seat at Sally and Audrey's dining room table. Bewilderment was stamped across the broad planes of his face.

Letty couldn't quite hold her chuckle.

"You have something you want to say?" His voice was rich

molasses that... comforted. It held the warmth of familiarity without the baggage of actual memories. How had she not noticed his voice before?

She shook her head. "Nope. Not a thing."

Audrey climbed up the back of Dawson's chair to drop a flowered hat on his head. It clashed terribly with the big lacy apron she'd made him put on and the gaudy purple necklace that he'd had to wrap around himself three times before it was short enough not to be a tripping hazard. On Audrey, it would have been wrapped ten times, easy.

"Thank you." His soft words were for the little girl who had just poured him a cup of imaginary tea.

When he picked up his cup, though, Audrey corrected him. "No, no, no! You have t' stick yoh pinky out." She demonstrated, channeling her inner royalty.

"No yelling at guests, daughter of mine!" Sally's shout came from the kitchen where she was making sandwiches.

Letty would have normally helped Sally, but she hadn't been able to tear her eyes away from Dawson as he got hit by a four-year-old tornado of determined domesticity.

"Saw-wee! I didn't mean to huht yoh feelings." Audrey's eyes grew three times their normal size as she looked at Dawson in apology.

He leaned toward the girl. "All's forgiven. Now show me what you mean about my pinky."

Audrey clambered onto the table and sat cross-legged by Dawson's teacup, carefully wrapping his fingers around the handle and bending his pinky out at the perfect angle. Once she was satisfied, she climbed back down to her seat and gave him a regal nod. "Jus' like that."

Dawson's eyes twinkled. "Ah. Now I see what I was doing wrong. Thank you for showing me."

Audrey beamed at him before pouring her own cup of air-tea. "One lump, or two?"

"One, please."

She picked up the tiny metal tongs and pretended to select a sugar cube from the empty sugar bowl before gently placing it into his cup. "Have to be ca'ful not to splash."

"Of course."

"Cweam?"

Dawson considered the cream pitcher. "I don't usually put cream in my tea. What do you suggest?"

It shouldn't have been possible for Audrey's smile to grow any wider, but it somehow did. "I like cweam in my tea, but it's okay if you don't. No judgmen'."

"I guess I can give it a try. If you think it's good, I'm sure I'll like it."

The four-year-old stretched her arms as far as they could go to pretend-pour cream into Dawson's cup. Then she sank onto her knees, too short to sit normally at the table. She lifted her cup to her lips and drank daintily before giving her companion a nod. "Is it to yoh satsfaction?"

She wouldn't be able to swallow her smile much longer, so Letty finally moved toward the kitchen to see if Sally needed her. Before she stepped out of the dining room, though, she heard Dawson's reply.

"Scrumptious. Absolutely scrumptious."

9

Even though Dawson saw Letty most nights because of the play, it wasn't enough. Something about Letty tugged at him. She was magnetic in the most unassuming way, and it wasn't just him. She didn't see the way people watched her, how they were drawn to her.

He noticed it because he'd developed the habit of eating lunch at Heavenly Brew. He got in his fair share of Letty-watching time. Which meant he'd already had plenty of practice watching the way people were drawn to her and how they walked away with a lighter step after talking to her. He didn't skulk around the shop or anything like that. He just... enjoyed being in her orbit. Being around Letty filled his dark corners with light. She shone a light in the shadows he still harbored. What's more, she made him want to welcome light into the shadows he'd been hiding behind ever since...

He shut the thought down before it finished. No need to go there.

Better to just focus on life in Gilead and the puzzle that was Letty Stanton.

The temperatures outside might rival Siberia in the dead of

winter, but his day wasn't complete without a walk to the coffee shop and the chance to sit, eat, and watch. Heavenly Brew overflowed with an intoxicating kind of peace, and it was all due to Letty. She was the reason the shop did such good business. The coffee and food were good, but they weren't enough to make most people brave the winter weather.

Dawson had just polished off his bacon and egg salad sandwich when his phone rang. "Hey, Mom. How's your day?"

"Lovely, dear. And even better now that I've heard your voice. How's the new job?"

"I thought I'd hate it after that first meeting with HR, but it's proving to be more captivating than I expected."

"Captivating, huh? That's an... interesting way to describe one's job. What about the Easter play? Is it going okay?" She wasn't asking about the play. She was asking about him and how he was handling being part of an Easter play. She wasn't going to say that, though, in case he didn't want to talk about it. Mom could do tact and grace like nobody else he'd ever met.

"It's... okay. I've been distracted by other things, and after that initial gut punch, it's been... okay. Fine, even."

"I'm so glad to hear that. You know you can call if you ever need to talk about it."

"I know. And appreciate it."

"I wasn't actually calling about the play. I did some asking around, and none of my Chicago friends seem to know your Letty."

His Letty. He liked the sound of that. His eyes found her where she moved fluidly behind the counter taking orders and helping with meal prep. "Don't worry about it, Mom. No need to keep asking."

"Oh. Okay. Not... interested... anymore?"

Ha. Mom couldn't be more wrong if she tried. He couldn't get what Letty'd said out of his mind, though. Wherever she'd been before Gilead hadn't been safe. He needed to know more before he poked too hard at something and stirred up a whole mess of hurt. How to explain all that to his mom, though? If he said any of that, she'd be like a dog with a bone — unable to let it go. She couldn't stand the thought of anyone hurting, even if it was long in the past — one of the many traits he'd inherited from her.

"Dawson?"

Ah. Yeah. She was still waiting for an answer. "Not interested in going behind someone's back to learn about their past."

"Hm. Okay. I'm not sure what to read into that."

A low chuckle slipped out as he watched Letty turn to put a plated sandwich on the counter, almost smacking her employee in the face with the plate. She shifted at the last second and avoided the collision like a pro. "Could you try not to read anything into it? Just this once?"

"I'll try. But it makes me want to come visit you in your new town."

"It'd be a boring visit. I work all day, and I'm stuck at rehearsals five out of seven nights."

"I have a feeling that somewhere in the midst of all that I'd find some things — or maybe some people — that are decidedly not boring. But fine. I won't plan a road trip just yet."

And... proverbial bullet dodged. "Love you, Mom."

"Love you more, kiddo. Let me know if you need anything."

"'Kay. Bye."

Dawson cleared his table, lifted a hand in farewell, and slipped back out into the bright winter day.

THE ACTING TROUPE hooted and hollered as they streamed into the auditorium. Dawson lifted an eyebrow in Letty's direction.

"It's still the first week. They're all hopped up on hope, dreams, and the victory of winning a part. They'll be tired of rehearsals soon enough."

One of the actors approached her table and grabbed a sandwich and soda. "What do I owe you?"

Letty gave the guy a smile. "It's on the house. Or on the college. They pay for it so you guys don't faint from hunger and thirst during rehearsals."

The guy — Connor, if memory served — gave her a funny look before nodding. "Well, thanks."

Dawson waited until the actor was a few yards away before asking, "Was that Jesus?"

Letty laughed. "It never stops getting weird when people say things like that. But yeah, he's playing Jesus."

"Thank goodness. I wasn't sure what we were going to do if we ended up with that 'It is finished' guy for the part."

"Hm. So it's 'we' now, is it?"

He gave her a shrug. "If you can't beat 'em..."

"You get over your Easter hang-up yet?"

"Maybe? I don't know. I still don't..." He trailed off, not sure how to voice all the mixed-up feelings inside his heart.

"It's okay. You don't have to tell me." Her voice held no judgment, and her eyes — they were filled with the kind of understanding born of pain. Even if they *were* also laced with curiosity.

"Yeah. Maybe..." He took a deep breath and let it out. "Thanks."

She smiled before turning her attention to the next thirsty thespian. "What'll it be?"

"You have any kombucha?"

Dawson snorted. Kombucha? At a college play's rehearsal. The world sure had changed since he'd been a student.

"We have kombucha in the shop, but we don't stock it for

rehearsal. Come by Heavenly Brew sometime during the week, though, and check out our selection. We have some fun flavors. Would you like something else?"

"Uh... yeah. I'll just grab a Coke. Thanks."

Dawson looked over at the drink selection. Not that he'd say kids today were spoiled — because that would make him sound old — but... "Think she'll stop by to check out your kombucha?"

"Fifty-fifty, but if she does stop in, she'll probably walk out with a triple mocha or something like that."

"You that good at reading people?"

She tapped her temple near her right eye. "Years of experience at work here. I see what people really mean when they say crazy things like kombucha."

He didn't doubt a word of it. "So what's your idea of a fun flavor?"

"We have a pink grapefruit that's pretty good, and a spicy ginger one that has a nice bite. But we also have cotton candy, candied apple, and sour gummy bear flavors. They're more popular than I expected when we first decided to give the kombucha craze a try. Cotton candy and gummy bear, especially, are hard to keep in stock."

"Kids today..." Yeah, there was no help for it. He sounded...

"Are you going for geriatric there? Or...?"

"What can I say? I'm an old soul."

Letty burst into laughter, and lightning might as well have struck straight through his heart. The shock froze him in place as electricity raced to all his nerve endings and back again.

Nicolette Stanley.

Nicki.

Not Letty. Not Stanton.

Nicki Stanley.

He did know her.

He knew her well.

She might not remember him, but she was the first girl he'd ever fallen head over heels for. Back then, she had been... The most stunning girl. The sweetest smile. The kindest eyes. The most beautiful laugh. Everything. She had been everything.

How had he not seen it sooner?

"Yo. Dawson. Everything okay?"

He shook his head and tried to pull himself back into the present.

"Dawson. Hey! The director's calling you."

He turned away from Letty — Nicki — and looked toward the front of the auditorium where one of the directors was waving his arms and speaking into the mic on his headset.

Oops. Volume. Volume was good.

Which knob was it again?

10

L etty turned from Dawson to the guy walking away from her table. "One sandwich next time, please. I'm not your three squares a day."

The kid tossed a sheepish look over his shoulder before he gave her a nod and went on his way.

Her gaze roamed back over to Dawson. He'd gotten the director's mic turned on and was turning knobs and pushing faders on the sound board, but he still looked like he was only about ten percent present.

He made Casper look downright tanned by comparison, too.

"Hey. Dawson. Everything okay?"

He didn't even look her way, let alone respond. His headphones were MIA, too.

Well, then.

A hollow twisty feeling worked its way through her stomach.

It'd been a long time since someone had been able to stoke her insecurities and hurt her like that.

She must like Dawson more than she'd realized.

Liking people was dangerous. When you liked someone, you gave them the power to influence you. And to cause you pain.

Letty dragged her eyes away from Dawson and busied herself with tidying up the refreshment table.

Her attention stayed with the man in the sound booth even though she forced her gaze into submission like an angry overlord with an unruly vassal.

Forward. She needed to keep her gaze forward.

Dawson hadn't stopped in at Heavenly Brew on Saturday. He'd been a no-show at Sunday's church service. He didn't come in for lunch on Monday, either.

Now it was Monday night, and a college student, barely a man, stood at the sound booth. A deer with somebody's headlights bearing down on him had nothing on the shaggy-haired kid.

"Uh. Hey. Do you know how to turn this on?" The hope in his eyes was almost Letty's undoing.

She walked over to stare at the space. "Well, he usually flips a switch somewhere over here..." She waved her hand in the general area. "Then he toggles something on the back. Then he starts messing with the settings."

The college student, who still looked like he was years away from his first shave, stared hard at the spot where Letty had waved her hand. "Somewhere over here?"

"Yeah. Sorry. That's the best I can do."

He flipped a switch, and some of the equipment lit up. He did a fist pump before reaching around to find the toggle switch on the back. "Thanks for the help. I can probably figure it out from here."

"Where's... uh... Dawson?"

The kid didn't spare her a look as he continued to study the sound board. "Dunno. This is only my second day, and all I've done so far is help the profs get their computers to communicate with their classroom projectors. This stuff here is next level. Maybe I'll get a raise since I'm covering for him."

"What do you mean, you don't know? You knew enough to be here."

"Yeah. He just texted and asked if I could take his shift tonight. Didn't say why, though."

Oh. That wasn't exactly helpful information.

"Hey, you think I could get one of those drinks?"

"Sure. What'll it be?"

"Got any kombucha?"

"Have you thought about using one of those online dating sites? I hear they're not all sleazy."

Letty accepted Mrs. Butler's ten-dollar bill and made change for her. "Heavenly Brew keeps me pretty busy. I don't really have time for a boyfriend."

"Ah, but if you married, you'd have someone to share the work with you."

"Either that, or I'd end up taking on half of his work on top of all my own."

Mrs. Butler shook her head. "Someday, dear, you'll find yourself in my shoes — old and alone. The memories of the people you've loved will be the only company you have some days, so make sure you store up plenty of them."

Letty had plenty of memories, and Letty had known love. She's also known heart-wrenching pain. She'd known betrayal, too. She had zero desire to repeat those experiences. Mrs. Butler didn't need to hear any of that, though. So Letty gave her a nod. "I'm glad you have those memories, but any time you want some real live company, feel free to stop on in. You're always welcome here."

The seventy-something woman turned toward the door but then stopped and looked back. "Do you mean that?"

"I wouldn't have said it otherwise."

Mrs. Butler smiled at her, then turned to go take a seat at one of the tables rather than taking her drink out the door like usual.

Letty turned to the next customer and offered a smile she was sure didn't reach her eyes. "What can I get for you today?"

Order after order. Letty fell into the comfortable predictability of her job. Some of the college kids she'd hired in the past would say the job was monotonous, and that was why they couldn't stick with it. It wasn't exciting enough. Not interesting enough. Or... just plain not enough. Letty liked the sameness of the routine, though. She never got bored, either, because each new person who came in brought a new twist to her day.

Take Mrs. Butler, for example. After she finished her coffee, the woman walked right behind the order counter and stored her purse. Letty stared at her, mouth hanging open, as the woman pushed her way into the kitchen. Within moments, the sound of humming drifted out through the swinging doors. Letty tiptoed over to the kitchen door and peaked through the little window. Mrs. B was wearing an apron and washing dishes.

Huh. It was one thing when Dawson pitched in and helped. He was young and strong and... all Dawson-y. Mrs. B, though, was frail and old and... willing. And maybe a little lonely. When it came down to it, though, Mrs. B wouldn't wash dishes unless she wanted to.

Letty backed away from the door and continued taking orders while Cici filled them. She only blinked a few times, too, when Mrs. B exited the kitchen and carried a bucket of cleaning supplies over to the restrooms to clean them.

Could she afford another employee? Time was always a

limited commodity during rehearsals for the college's Easter play. Another pair of hands would be nice.

Two hours after she'd deposited her purse behind the counter, Mrs. Butler collected it, gave Letty a wave, and walked out the front door without a word.

She'd look at the books again as soon as she got the chance. Surely she could find the funds to pay Mrs. Butler if the woman wanted to come back and help her.

LETTY'S STEP faltered as she walked into the auditorium.

Dawson stood at the sound booth, his back to her. His normal relaxed posture was gone. His shoulders were tight, his back stiff.

What was she supposed to say to the man? He'd ghosted her.

Yeah, yeah. That was an extreme description.

It'd only been a few days. But, still. It had felt like ghosting. Like he'd suddenly decided she didn't matter.

And as much as she didn't want to give in to the thoughts, a part of her wondered if she *did* matter. His actions, even though he probably hadn't meant them to, had caused a kajillion old insecurities to resurface.

She belonged to Christ. He found value in her. She knew that. She did.

But... outside of His perfect love for her, it kind of seemed sometimes like people would be better off without her. Or, at least, they wouldn't be any worse off without her. Like she could disappear, and the world would just keep on spinning. A few people might notice her absence, but nobody would really miss her. Life would keep going for everyone as though she'd never been a part of it.

Letty shook her head, trying to dislodge the dark thoughts.

Sometimes her past sank its unforgiving talons into her psyche. It took a lot of time and mental energy to peel them away. It took fortitude — something she didn't seem to have at the moment.

She brought the dolly to a stop and reached for the top crate, the one with the sandwiches. She refused to look at the man next to her.

Before she could latch onto the handholds, though, to heave the crate up, another pair of hands got there. Big manly hands with a dusting of hair across their backs.

"Here, let me get that."

11

D awson set the crate onto the table and reached for the next one.

Letty stood there, staring at him with a bottomless gaze.

He tried again. "Hey."

She blinked a couple of times before replying. "Hey."

Her eyes gave nothing away, but that one word left him with freezer burn. It wasn't cold, exactly. It was the absence of warmth. He might not have noticed if he hadn't become so accustomed to Letty's special brand of warmth. No one would ever accuse her of running around and randomly handing out hugs. She had a way about her, though, the kind of kindness that seeped in through the cracks in a person's armor and thawed all the cold places they hadn't even realized they'd had.

Hers was the kind of warmth that had staying power, and its lack hurt.

He owed her something. "Sorry I've been a little absent."

"No problem. You don't owe me anything."

He took the airpot filled with coffee from her hands and set it on the table. "But I feel like I do."

"Well, you don't."

"Letty—"

She cut him off without apology. "I think the director wants you."

DAWSON DEALT with the director's request before returning to the relative solitude of his sound booth.

Letty dealt with a steady stream of hungry and thirsty members of the cast and crew. Busy enough that she didn't need to actively avoid him. It happened naturally.

He scrubbed a hand down his face. It didn't matter how much he wished it, he couldn't go back and change the past. As soon as he'd realized he really did recognize Letty, he'd shut down. She was hiding something. They weren't exactly BFFs, but he'd still felt lied to. Betrayed.

It didn't matter that she probably had no idea who he was. He couldn't change the shock and hurt he'd felt.

He'd sat at his dining room table Friday night, after mindlessly driving home from rehearsal, and wondered how she'd managed to dupe him. Had she known all along who he was? Did she remember their shared past? Was she going home each evening and laughing at his expense? At him?

He'd woken up Saturday with a clearer head. He might not know this new version of Letty as well as he would like, but nothing in her behavior toward anyone could lead him to believe she was malicious.

So Dawson and his laptop had spent Saturday and Sunday investigating every article they could find about Nicolette Stanley.

And what he'd found had torn his heart in two.

His family had moved from San Francisco to Chicago when

he'd been a sophomore in high school. His puppy love infatuation with Nicki hadn't stopped overnight, but lack of opportunity had put a damper on it until it had eventually faded into the obscure recesses of his mind.

It was weird how, when you moved away and didn't see another person for years, that person was frozen in time. Even though he logically knew his Nicki had grown up and gone out into the world, in his mind, she was perpetually fifteen, uncorrupted by the real world or the hardships of life.

The reality, though, was so very different.

Two years after his family left San Francisco, Nicki's world had fallen apart. All her social media accounts had gone silent, too. In a single day, her life had imploded, and she'd essentially disappeared from the face of the earth.

Pictures of Letty's mom still made the paper, but the pictures of their entire family that had once regularly graced the society section were no more.

Her dad had died in a car accident with an unnamed underaged driver behind the wheel. Then Letty — or Nicki — was gone.

Had she run away? Or been exiled?

What she'd said about Philip's place being safe... Had he read too much into it? She hadn't come right out and said that her life before Gilead had been unsafe.

And yet... he knew.

Call it gut feeling. Call it discernment. Call it whatever.

He just *knew*.

Something terrible had happened to Nicki, and she'd been forced to reinvent herself. She'd become Letty, and she'd been in Gilead ever since.

Letty's dad had doted on her, and she'd adored him. Whether it was on the golf course, sharing a dance at a fundraiser, or career day at school — nobody could have missed it. The two of them had shared a bond.

Losing him — regardless of the circumstances — had to have crushed her. What on earth happened on top of that, though, to make her run and never look back? How did someone from San Francisco's upper echelon end up homeless in a Kansas bus depot? Where had her mother been? How could she have allowed her daughter to land in such a precarious position? Anything could have happened to Nicki. To Letty.

Anything. And the thought made him sick.

The more he thought about it, the more he wanted to demand answers.

He couldn't, though.

Letty was too skittish. He couldn't risk pushing her away any more than he already had. And he needed to find a way to bridge the gap he'd created between them.

Somehow. Some way.

He tried to rid himself of the memories so Letty couldn't read them in his eyes, but it was nearly impossible.

DAWSON SLIPPED through the door at Heavenly Brew. The jingle of the bell drew Letty's eyes, but then she turned away and escaped into the kitchen.

The teen girl — Cici, if he recalled — took his order. When she served it to him, Dawson took the food and drink and found his way to a back corner table. If he sat where she couldn't spot him...

Sure enough, after a few minutes, Letty left the kitchen and made her way back into the coffee shop proper. She took her place at the register and helped another couple of customers before there was a lull and her gaze wandered over her coffee house domain.

She couldn't hide her cringe when she noticed him still there.

That kind of hurt.

Oh, well. He'd done it to himself.

"Hey, Letty."

She nodded in his direction before busying herself with polishing the pristine display case.

Dawson finished his lunch, tied his scarf back around his neck, and pulled his hat and gloves on. As he headed toward the exit, he tipped his hat. "Have a nice day, ladies."

Dawson arrived early at the auditorium. He was going to help Letty unload the evening's food and drinks whether she wanted him to or not.

Until Philip pushed the heavily loaded dolly through the door.

"No Letty tonight?"

"Nope."

"She busy?"

"Nope."

"You're a great conversationalist, you know that?"

Philip gave him a sage nod. "Yep."

Dawson ate lunch at Heavenly Brew every day that week.

Letty avoided Dawson while he was at Heavenly Brew every day that week.

Dawson showed up early to rehearsal every single night.

Philip showed up on time to rehearsal every single night.

But then Saturday came. Maybe Letty would be shorthanded at the coffee shop. He could drop in oh-so-casually — even though he wasn't going to be fooling anyone — and see if she needed any help.

When Dawson stepped into the bustling coffee shop, though, Letty was far from alone. A college student he'd seen around rehearsals was working the register, Letty was filling orders, and a spritely older lady in a hot pink floral apron was bussing tables.

Discouraged but not daunted, he got in line and waited his turn.

"Psst. Is that the guy Letty likes?"

Dawson had no idea where the whispered question had come from, but when he looked up, most everyone in Heavenly Brew was staring straight at him. They all quickly averted their gazes.

"Sh. Not so loud."

"I don't think she likes him, anyway."

"So sad."

The whispers floated around the dining room, circling him from different directions without really telling him who was doing the talking. Or maybe telling him that everyone was part of the conversation.

"He'd be perfect for her."

"You can't know that."

"He's single and under fifty."

"Hmph. He can't be the only man in town who's single and under fifty."

"No, but he's the only one who's in here six days a week."

Someone snorted at that remark before being shushed.

"Can I help you?"

Dawson forced his attention to the young woman taking his

order. "A slice of the ham Florentine quiche, please. And a large dark roast hot coffee for here."

She confirmed his order, let him pay, and handed him a mug for his coffee and a plate with his quiche on it.

He stopped at the coffee station and fixed his drink the way he wanted it before moving on to a table by the front window. It gave him a perfect view of where Letty was working. Something about seeing her bustling around in her little corner of the world soothed him.

He might have made a mess of things, but he hadn't given up hope.

"He's got it bad."

"So sad it's not mutual."

"You kidding? The way she's avoiding looking at him? It's definitely mutual."

Dawson shook his head. He thought of himself as a private person. Living in Gilead, though, was teaching him a few things. One, privacy was an illusion. Two, maybe that wasn't such a bad thing after all.

When he was halfway through his quiche, hot pink moved into his line of sight and blocked his view of the front counter. He looked up — not very far — at the elderly woman standing over him. "Can I help you?"

"I'm just cleaning." She proceeded to wipe down the only other chair at his table. Three times.

"I think it's probably clean now."

"Can't be too sure."

"Um. Unless you're cleaning it with mud, I think we can be pretty sure."

Her eyes scolded him for talking back. "Some things take a little time. You have to do the job with care. Can't go trying once and then calling it quits and assuming the chair's all clean. The chair's not going to tell me if it's clean, is it? So I can't give up. Just have to keep at it, nice and gentle like."

And the third thing he'd learned about life in a small town? Some people were just flat-out crazy. "Do the chairs normally talk to you? You know, to tell you if they're clean or not?"

She gave him a hard glare. "It's not about being clean. It's about making sure you're not an imbecile who thinks the job's done when it's not."

Then, bless her, she shifted her eyes over to where Letty stood before looking back at Dawson with that same hard glare.

"Ah. We're not talking about chairs, are we?"

"You might be the densest boy I've ever met, and that's saying something. I taught middle school for forty years."

Laughter burst from Dawson before he could stop it, and every eye in the restaurant — including Letty's — was back on him.

The woman shook her head, but her glare softened the tiniest bit. "You treat her wrong, and half this town will be ready to gut you like a fresh fish at supper time."

"That seems a bit... violent."

She tsked. "You should see what we do to day-old fish."

12

L etty tried to sneak into her Sunday school class, but Walter, the teacher, was having none of that. "Hey, Letty! Come on in. There's a seat over by Dawson. You know him, right?"

If the floor opened up and swallowed her whole, she probably wouldn't complain. Since the floor kept its gaping maw closed, though, she had no choice but to fall into the seat next to the man she was doing everything in her power to avoid.

"Good morning." His voice was far too attractive. Why couldn't he have a nasally voice? Or some sort of high-pitched squeaky voice that made her think of rats? No, no. He had to have a voice like baklava — the perfect amount of crisp drowned in honey and laced with all kinds of decadent goodness.

Jerk.

She crossed her arms, gave him a brief nod so people wouldn't think she was rude, and turned her attention to the front of the class.

About halfway through class, though, everything got way too interesting.

"We're going to do something a little different today." Walter gave his hands a single clap.

Was he trying to convince the class to be enthusiastic? He was a good teacher, but he didn't usually do anything too terribly unpredictable...

"Pair up with the person next to you. I'm going to give you five minutes to talk about something in your life that God has redeemed — something you thought was awful but that He worked out for good. We don't have time to go around the whole class and do this, but I want you to have the benefit of hearing each other's stories."

Letty turned to her left, but Shauna's back was already to her. That left her with...

"I guess it's you and me." Absurd honey-pastry voice.

She stared at the man next to her. She'd give anything not to have this conversation. Not with him. Not with anyone. She didn't like talking about her past. Her life. Herself.

Her heart raced, and her palms grew damp.

If she claimed a panic attack to get out of this exercise, she wouldn't even have to fake it.

"Why don't I go first?"

Letty tugged her head down in a semblance of a nod. She could probably get through this if she avoided eye contact. Dawson didn't need to be peeking into the depths of her soul. Or whatever part of it her eyes might let leak out.

"I was engaged. Her name was Jayla. She told me once that it meant 'God will protect.' Only He didn't protect her. At least not the way I wanted Him to."

Letty couldn't keep her eyes down. She met Dawson's gaze and saw his turmoil there. It was tempered by time, but she recognized the pain of loss.

"We were on our way home from Easter church service, and we were caught up in a collision. It was the dumbest thing. Too much traffic pouring out of the church. All those people who only attend once or twice a year, you know? And somebody out on the road wasn't paying attention to their red light. They just blew through it and plowed into the line of cars inching their way out of the church."

"I'm so sorry." She couldn't let his pain go unnoticed, unacknowledged.

"You know how when the car next to you starts going, you start to go, too, even if the light's still red?"

She gave him a solemn nod.

"When it was all said and done, twenty cars were tangled up in that mess. Everyone said it was such a blessing that there was only one fatality. Only one death in all that mess and mayhem. God's protection, they said."

Before she even knew what she was doing, Letty reached out and rested her hand on his where it lay fisted on his knee. She didn't have words. Not more than she'd already given him. Sometimes pain just needed to be left alone. Witnessed, but not pushed. People needed to be allowed to feel their pain without the platitudes meant to cover it up and hide it away like a dirty little secret.

"I still don't much like Easter, and I may never actually attend an Easter church service again. I don't really know. But even so, God redeemed it." Dawson ran his other hand down his face before meeting her eyes again and giving her a sad smile. "I wish it had never happened. I wish Jayla had lived a long and beautiful life. Her twin brother Jensen, her only sibling — he'd battled addiction for years. When she died, though, and he saw what it did to their parents, he fell to his knees and cried out to God. He'd always known he was heading toward death but hadn't really cared. He didn't want his parents to go through losing another child, though. So he begged God for help. He's been in recovery for three years now, and he's... doing good. He's faithful. He's growing. He's learning. He's a blessing to his family, to his church, and to everyone who knows him."

Letty swiped at the tears leaking from her eyes.

Dawson's voice wrapped around her. "In Jensen, God redeemed Jayla's death. It doesn't really make it hurt any less. But He worked it for good, you know? He took a terrible thing, and He brought from it something that Jayla had been praying for... for years. She loved her brother so much, and it would make her so happy to see where he is and how he's doing today."

"What a gift that you can see God at work even in the midst of such heartache."

A wry smile tugged at his lips. "Don't get me wrong. I didn't exactly see things that way at first. It took me a little while. But God is patient."

Letty pulled in a deep breath. Dawson had gone and shared a big, deep hurt in his life. He'd given her a piece of his truth. She couldn't very well return it with the story about the time someone broke into the shop and stole the day-old pastries. "I, uh..."

"All right, everyone. Good job! Eyes back on me, and we'll move forward with the lesson. Without giving me any specifics about the stories you shared with each other, can anyone tell me what you learned about God's redemptive power?"

Frank, sitting in the back of the class, spoke up. "God doesn't just redeem us when we accept Christ. His redemption is at work in us every day of our lives in big and little ways."

"Amen!" Walter nodded with a smile.

Shauna leaned forward in her chair. "When we're walking in Christ, we are wholly redeemed — every piece and part of our lives, every breath. We are redeemed for His purpose and His glory."

Walter nodded. "I couldn't have said it better myself."

Letty fought to keep her eyes off Dawson as she spoke.

"Redemption doesn't make the past go away. It takes it and puts it to a better use, though."

Walter gave her a thoughtful look. "Indeed. Our painful experiences shape us. When we let God redeem those experiences, we are shaped for the better. We're given a witness, a special compassion, a way to reach people we might not have been able to reach otherwise. When we hold tight to those painful experiences, though, and refuse to let God get His hands on them, we let bitterness grow and take root in our heart. We can't escape the painful experiences in our past, but we can choose to give them to God and leave them in His hands."

As class wrapped up and everyone began filtering out into the hallway, Letty took her time putting her Bible away and collecting the few items she'd brought with her into class. When they were alone in the room, she turned to face Dawson. "I'm sorry I've been giving you the cold shoulder. I just... I guess I have things in my past that I haven't totally let God redeem. I don't want to be a bitter person, though. So... I'm sorry."

Dawson reached out and brushed the backs of his fingers against her cheek. The touch was fleeting and feather-light. "Something came up that knocked me sideways, and I needed to figure out how to cope with it. I retreated while I sorted that out. I didn't realize I was hurting you when I did that. I couldn't quite see past the thing I was trying to deal with. I didn't mean to hurt you."

She gave a one-shouldered shrug as she turned for the door.

"I'm sorry for disappearing like I did. I'll try to be more thoughtful in the future."

Letty paused in the open doorway, not turning to face the man behind her. "You didn't owe me anything then, and you don't owe me anything now."

"But what if I'd like to? What if I'd like to be in the kind of friendship where it's normal that we loop each other in when something's going on?"

She chewed her bottom lip as she mulled over his words. Did she want to be tied to another person like that? Those kinds of ties hadn't always paid off for her in the past.

What am I supposed to do, God?

Something settled inside her soul — almost as if something out of alignment had finally clicked into place. A sense of rightness swept through her soul as warmth filled and tingled in her veins.

Letty turned to give Dawson her full attention. "I'm willing to try. I'll probably overreact to things sometimes. Like I might have overreacted to your absence. But I don't want to let the baggage from my past continue to control my future. I'll try."

Dawson's eyes brightened with an inner light that fueled that sense of rightness in her core. It was almost like...

Like coming home.

13
___

The week flew by like nobody's business. Nightly rehearsals were taking their toll on him, but Dawson was determined to be there every single night. If Letty could do it while running a business, then he could do it while working a full-time job. Besides which, being at rehearsal kind of was his job. Even if watching the same play rehearsed night after night after night got to be a bit monotonous.

It didn't matter if he did sometimes find his job boring at times. Letty made everything more interesting.

There was something about her.

There were so many things about her.

He wasn't a fool. He knew he was falling. Falling hard, too, and it didn't really make sense. He wasn't an impulsive guy. He was a think-it-through-from-all-angles kind of guy.

Of course, the way he ended up at Gilead made a mockery of that.

Maybe he was impulsive sometimes. Or not as thorough. Or...

Maybe it was all just God at work in his life. God was

sovereign, after all, wasn't He? And God wanted good things for His children.

Dawson had let himself get entrenched in his grief. He hadn't looked for a way out. He hadn't really considered the possibility that God might have someone for him, someone other than Jayla. A part of his heart had been buried with her.

His heart kept beating, though. And lately it seemed to be beating — at least partly — for Letty.

He kept noticing little things, too, that reminded him of the girl she used to be. Nicolette. Nicki. Sometimes it was hard to reconcile Letty and Nicki in his mind, and other times it was so clear he didn't understand how he hadn't immediately seen it.

Which was its own set of problems. He was eventually going to tell her.

He needed to.

Keeping what he knew a secret was... expedient. And dishonest.

How was he supposed to tell her, though?

Seriously? How did one broach that kind of subject?

Hey, you know how you used to live in San Francisco and go by a different name? Funny thing about that...

Dawson pushed the thoughts down as he swung open the door to Heavenly Brew. It was Saturday morning, and he fully intended to ingratiate himself to Letty by being completely indispensable.

You know, because nothing said romance like washing dishes and sweeping floors.

Only, as the door swung closed behind him, Dawson realized that he wasn't really needed. Letty had a young woman taking orders. She looked familiar. From the play, maybe? He didn't have a life, so it wasn't like he could run into people in too many places. He had to know her from the play. Janda? Joelle? Jenn? Jess... That was it. Jess. The one who didn't think it was at all weird to use the words *hot* and *disciples* in the same sentence.

While Jess was taking orders and Letty was making the drinks, the older woman with the bright pink apron was bustling around wiping the tables down and smiling as she did so.

Hm.

He could always offer to clean the bathrooms. That was sure to win him some points.

Or...

"This isn't a tourist attraction, you know." The pink-aproned woman looked up at him with fire — and maybe a touch of laughter — twinkling in her eyes. "Either get in line to order or find something else to do, but don't just stand around gawking."

Even with her white hair piled atop her head, the woman couldn't be much more than four and a half feet tall. And, going by the few interactions he'd had with her, every inch of her was packed with personality. "I planned to see if Letty needed any help."

Her mouth dropped open for the barest of seconds before she snapped it closed and nodded. "Best get yourself something to eat then. I'm sure I can find somewhere else to be when you're ready to get to work."

"I don't meant to..."

"Nonsense. By the time you're done with breakfast, I'll be ready to put my feet up in the breakroom."

"There's a breakroom?"

She pointed a manicured finger to his usual lunchtime table. "Obviously."

Dawson shook his head as he moved to get into line. A lot could be said about Gilead, Kansas, but nobody would ever say the town lacked character.

When it was his turn to order, he smiled at the young

woman behind the register. "I'd like an avocado bacon breakfast wrap and a large hot chai latte, extra chai, please."

"Hey, there."

Dawson looked up from the mixing bowl he was scouring. "Hey."

Letty nodded to the sink full of hot water. "Thank you for washing dishes."

"Happy to help."

Her eyes cast around the room as though looking for a topic. "You've been in for lunch every day this week."

"Where else would I eat?"

"Some people bring their lunch to work."

"Sounds overrated to me."

She studied her fingernails.

"Did you want to talk to me about something?" He tried not to stare, but it wasn't easy.

Her eyes widened and color stained her cheeks.

He lifted his hands in surrender. "No pressure."

Letty continued staring at her hands. "What do you think about maybe... um... maybe going to lunch tomorrow? After church."

Hold the horses, the phones, and everything in between. Did she just ask him out on a date? "Tomorrow?"

"Um, you know. If you want to. No biggie."

"I'd love to."

"Oh. Okay. Well, then. Okay."

She slipped out of the kitchen as quietly as she'd entered, and Dawson was left staring at the swinging doors as they closed. He smiled at his water-wrinkled hands. "I should wash dishes more often."

CHURCH HAD ENDED, and people were streaming into the main aisles and making their way toward the exits.

Dawson and Letty hadn't exchanged more than a few words during Sunday school, and he hadn't seen her at all during the worship service. If they were supposed to go out together, she'd need to show up eventually.

Unless... ugh. She wasn't going to stand him up, was she?

"Dawson! Dawson!"

His attention flew to the little girl racing toward him, two matching braids flying behind her.

"You coming to lunch at ou' house! Come on! Come on!" Audrey grabbed his hand with a surprisingly strong grip and started tugging him toward the door.

"Lunch? At your house?"

"Letty said she ak-sed you. Did you fo'get aw'eady?"

Ahhh.

Not a date.

How presumptuous of him.

And foolish.

Yep. He was an idiot. An idiot who was letting his — ugh — feelings get the better of him.

Bright eyes looked up at him. "You don't want to go to my house?"

He gave Audrey his biggest smile. "Where else could I possibly want to go?"

Her lips turned down the tiniest bit.

"Lead the way."

Her smile returned, and her voice boomed through the nearly empty sanctuary. "Come on, then! Lunch won't make itself!"

"So, on a scale of one to ten, who makes better coffee?" Sally looked at Dawson, eyebrow lifted.

"I'm not even sure that's a scalable question. There are only two possible answers."

Sally sighed dramatically. "Fine, fine. On a scale of one to ten, how much better is my coffee than Letty's?"

Dawson looked from her to Letty and back again. "Um. Do I get kicked out if I give an honest answer?"

Sally burst into laughter before shooting a look at Letty. "Someday I'm going to find a man who prefers my coffee, and when I do, I'm marrying the fool."

Letty chuckled. "Calling him a fool before you even meet him might not be the best start to the relationship. Besides, would you really want a guy who has such bad taste?"

Both of Sally's eyebrows rose.

Dawson wasn't touching this conversation for anything.

Letty's eyes lit with laughter. "You don't need a man who prefers your coffee. You just need a man who prefers you."

"And who loves Jesus!" Audrey whisper-shouted — which was much more shout than whisper — as she entered the room carrying a small box of cards. "It's time for Exploding Kittens!"

Sally hung her head. "I thought you were getting Candyland."

"Everyone knows Exploding Kittens is more fun."

Letty's lips twitched.

Audrey shoved the box at Dawson. "Can you shuffle? Please? There's a goat. And kittens that go boom. And it's so much fun!"

Dawson took the box, removed the cards, and began shuffling. "Someone's going to have to explain this game to me."

Sally cut the deck for him. "Don't get killed by a kitten. There. Now you know how to play."

Letty's lip-twitch progressed to a full-face twitch that she tried to hide behind her hands.

"Are you okay, Letty? You look sick." Audrey's voice was painfully earnest.

"I'm... okay... just dandy... Nothing to see... here."

Dawson consulted the box to see how many cards he should deal.

Letty got control of herself with a deep breath. "Someday aliens are going to find this planet, and they're going to hear a soundbite about exploding kittens being fun, and they're going to either fly away at top speed or decide to take out the whole planet to save the universe — and the kittens — from our madness."

"Don't wo'y." Audrey patted her hand. "No kittens weally get hu't. It's only pwetend."

Letty grinned. "That's good to know. I was worried there for a minute about what your mom's been teaching you."

They were on the third round of cards when Dawson's phone rang with his mom's ringtone. "Hey. Do you mind? I should take this."

Sally and Letty waved him away. "Go ahead."

He stepped away from the dining table and into the living room. "Hey, Mom. What's up?"

"I think I found your friend."

Dawson's eyes flew back to the table where Letty was consulting with Audrey over which card she should play.

"Friend?"

"Do you remember the Stanleys? They had a daughter, Nicolette."

"Mom, I..." He paused to turn down the volume on his phone. He didn't need Letty hearing this. "Listen, Mom..."

"She disappeared. There was a scandal. Her dad died, and she vanished. The picture you sent me looks like her, and the age is about right. She used to go by Nicki, but Nicolette could be shortened to Letty, too. It makes sense."

Dawson tore a hand through his hair. "Okay, okay. Thanks, Mom."

"You're not interested?"

"I sort of already figured it out."

"When?"

"Not too long after we talked last time."

"Oh. Were you going to tell me?"

"I wasn't not telling you. I just... I'm just trying to figure things out."

His mom's silence wrapped him up in a blanket of guilt.

"I appreciate you calling. And everything else, too. It's just not a good time."

"Gotcha. Everything okay?"

He still had Letty in his line of sight. He didn't really want to stand anywhere that he couldn't see her. "Everything's good here. I'm sorry I didn't let you know I figured it out. I've just been... preoccupied."

"With Nicolette?"

"Maybe?"

"Should I be worried? The stories that people spread about her after she disappeared..."

"No. I don't know what the gossip says, but I know who she is right now, and you don't need to be worried. I'm good. Things are good."

"It's been a long time since..."

He finally turned his back on the dining room. "We're not dating, okay? But I like her, and I'm getting to know her. Things are complicated. But good, too."

He always knew when his mom was smiling. It was in her voice. This might have been a small smile, but it was a smile nonetheless. "Okay. I'm officially not worrying. But you'll catch me up on the details when you get a chance?"

"I will. I promise."

"'Kay. Love you."

"Love you, too."

When he returned to the table, Sally gave him an appraising look. "Lady friend?"

"Mom."

Sally and Letty exchanged a look before Sally turned to her daughter. "Let that be a lesson to you, young lady. You always answer the phone when your mom is calling."

Audrey rolled her eyes. "Why would I eve' not answer, Mommy? Duh."

14

L etty sat up in bed. Her Wednesday alarm hadn't gone off yet. There'd been a sound. Always a light sleeper, she'd woken easily at the noise. But what was it?

The wood-on-wood scrape met her ears, and her heart leapt into her throat. Someone was in the shop. She heard the sound of a chair moving on the floor hundreds of times each day. She knew that sound like she knew her own name.

Cell phone in hand, she debated. Investigate herself? Call the police?

Life in small-town middle America had softened her, but not so much that she didn't remember the ways of the world she'd fled when she came to Gilead.

But did she want there to be a record of a 911 call?

She only had one number on speed dial, and this was as good a time as any to use it.

"Thisbetterbegood." Philip's gruff voice instantly calmed Letty's racing heart.

"I think someone's in the shop."

"Call the police."

"I don't want... I don't... I..." She knew she was paranoid, but she usually tried to hide that from other people.

"On my way. Sit tight. Don't move or your floor creaking'll be heard downstairs."

The line was dead before she took her next breath. She sat on her bed, phone held in a death grip with fingers white enough to stand out in the night, arms wrapped around her knees. Her heart jumped and skittered around inside her chest.

It was nothing. It had to be nothing. It had been nothing for years now. It wasn't going to be something now after so many years of nothing.

It was nothing.

Everything was okay.

She was okay.

The shop was okay.

It was nothing.

Long before her heart was ready to calm, the telltale screech — something she really needed to get fixed — of the kitchen door met her ears. She held her breath, not wanting to miss a single sound. That made the bark of laughter easy to hear.

Philip was laughing. "Come on down, Letty-girl! I've got your intruder."

Laughter... At least she didn't call 911 and make a bigger fool of herself.

And... he wouldn't be laughing if it was something.

See? It was nothing. No reason to get worked up.

Letty made her way down the stairs from her apartment to the coffee shop below. The tables were all where they were supposed to be, but a few of the chairs were askew. And there was flour. Everywhere.

Flour. Every. Where.

A face popped around the corner from the kitchen, and a squeak escaped her lips before she could stop it. "Philip!" She gave his shoulder a shove. "What on earth happened down here? Was it teenagers?"

Philip just laughed again. "Your intruders are in the kitchen. Don't worry. They won't bite you."

Letty pushed through the swinging door to the kitchen and grunted at the sight before her. Two raccoons stared at her through the wire cage that was closed over the top of the industrial mixer. "You put them in the mixer!?"

Philip grunted. "Would you rather the fridge?"

The raccoons had ripped open a fifty-pound bag of flour... and maybe one pound of it was left in the remnants of the bag. The kitchen was covered in flour, the dining room had a dusting of it everywhere, and...

"We open in four hours..." She was supposed to start baking in one, but the entire kitchen and dining room would need to be cleaned and sanitized before she could even think about preparing for the morning rush.

"I called animal control, but Frank's tied up with some skunks. Apparently mating season got into full swing earlier than expected."

"Mating skunks? I..." Letty shook her head. "I don't want to know. I don't want to imagine."

Philip tucked his phone back into the holster on his belt. "Your predicament doesn't look nearly as bad when you compare this mess to what two amorous skunks could have done in here."

Letty fought the tug on her lips. "Who else can we call?"

"Can you call in a favor from anyone at the college? Maybe one of the actors you've been feeding is in the veterinary program or something."

"I don't even know if the Bible college has a vet program. But..." Letty snapped her fingers. "Penn! Let me check with her."

A nod from Philip. "I'll start cleaning up in the dining room, then."

With a nod, Letty ran back upstairs to change from pajamas into work clothes and to call Penelope, the gal in charge of the petting zoo and live animals for the Easter production. Hopefully she could help.

Letty almost gave up after the fifth ring, but a sleepy voice finally came on the line. "Who is this?"

"Hi. Uh, Penn. This is Letty. I handle the refreshments at rehearsal. We met..."

"Um, yeah. What time is it?"

"Two. Or so." Letty ran a hand down her face. "It's around two. I'm so sorry to call, but I didn't know who else could help."

Penn's voice got a little clearer. "Is everything okay?"

"Two raccoons busted into the coffee shop. I've got them trapped, but I don't know how to safely remove them or where to take them or anything."

"Did you try animal control?"

"Frank's dealing with a pair of mating skunks on someone's property."

The woman's bark of laughter was quick. "Again? That's the third time this week. Poor guy's probably going to be smelling skunk for months at the rate he's going."

"I... uh... yeah... about the raccoons..."

"Sure. Yeah, yeah. Give me twenty. Should I come to the front or the back?"

"The back's probably best. We're cleaning the dining room now, and I don't want the raccoons in there again if I can help it."

"See you soon."

The line went dead, and Letty stared at the phone in her hand. Rushing back into the dining room, she called out to Philip. "We need to sanitize —"

Philip rolled his eyes. "Everything. I was running this place long before you showed up and stole it from me."

That man's calm presence was probably the only thing preventing her complete meltdown. She'd be lucky if she could offer cinnamon rolls to people by the time she opened the doors. Philip wouldn't leave her to drown in the deep end, though. He was dependable like that.

"Can it, old man. It's not my fault the customers like me more than they like you."

"Old man? That the best you got? Not awake enough yet for a real insult, huh?" His chuckle soothed Letty's frazzled and ragged edges. Philip had always been good at that — taking the teeth out of her bite with kindness and humor. Fool old man.

The two fell into a long-established routine. Heavenly Brew may have been Philip's baby, but Letty had put a solid decade of blood, sweat, and tears into the place, too. He'd taught her everything he knew, and when he started thinking about retirement, he'd talked to her about transitioning the business to her. They were in that awkward place where they each owned fifty percent while she saved up the money to buy out the rest of it, but awkward was okay. It suited them. The way they'd first met had been kind of awkward, too.

She'd been alone, hungry — starving, really — and sleeping across two hard plastic molded bus depot chairs. She'd startled awake to find him cross-legged on the floor, a bag of coffee shop pastries in his hand, and earnestness in his eyes. She'd grabbed the pastries without hesitation when he'd held them out. She'd nearly choked trying to swallow them whole.

It was another three years, though, before she'd been willing to accept his sincerity and believe he really was who he seemed to be.

The best decision she'd ever made was entrusting herself — heart, soul, life, all of it — to Christ.

Trusting Philip had been the second-best decision of her life so far, though. And it was a decision she'd never regretted.

15

D awson jogged over to help Letty as soon as he saw her arrival at the auditorium doors. "Hey, there. You look..."

"Stunning and well rested?" The glare she threw his way was only half-hearted.

"Exactly what I was going to say." She looked like the walking dead, but that didn't seem like the kind of thing to throw at her.

"It's been a day."

"Yeah. Penn told me about your nocturnal visitors."

She shot him a look. "You guys hang out?"

He grabbed the heavy bags from her shoulders. "Nah. She thought I'd be interested, though, so she stopped by my office to tell me about your morning."

"And were you?"

"Was I..."

"Interested?" Her eyes widened, the aquamarine hue luminescent in the auditorium lights.

If he was a betting man, he'd bet she hadn't planned to say that at all. "Yes. Very."

Color swept her cheeks before her gaze dropped. She got to work setting out the sandwiches and muffins without giving him another look.

He pitched in to help her. "Do you know how they got in?"

She shrugged. "Kitchen door's been acting wonky. I meant to get it fixed. If I'd realized it was actually not latching properly, I'd have done something sooner."

He rested a hand on her forearm, stilling her movements. "With you living above the shop, I'm sure that had to be scary. I'm glad you're okay."

She still didn't make eye contact, but she nodded. "Thank you."

He'd take what he could get. Letty wasn't exactly the most emotionally transparent person he'd ever met. "If something like that comes up again, you know you can call me, right?"

She finally looked at him, her eyebrows drawn together. "Are we friends?"

Friends didn't keep secrets from each other, and they were both hiding things. What that meant for them in the future, he had no idea. Guilt surged inside him like a churning unsettled sea. "I'd like to think so. I'd at least like a chance to earn your friendship."

"That goes both ways, right? Two people earn each other's friendship?"

"Maybe, but I feel like I have more to prove."

"Hm." She looked toward the stream of people pouring into the auditorium for rehearsal before returning her gaze to his. "I guess I'm looking forward to that."

Such simple words, and somehow he felt like she'd just handed him the moon gift-wrapped and with a big bow. "Me, too."

REHEARSAL DREW TO A CLOSE, and the townies gathered at the back of the auditorium as they bundled into their coats. The college students descended on Letty's table like lions fresh off a hunger strike.

"Nicolette Stanley."

A voice carried over the crowd, its cultured tone not doing anything to put a dent in the noise. Even so, he'd heard it. And so had Letty, if her frozen movements were anything to go by.

"Nicolette, dear, lovely to see you after so long."

The crowd finally caught on to the fact that a bit of off-stage drama was unfolding in their midst. They parted to allow the woman in her stuffy suit, matching heels, and flawless face to pass.

Letty still hadn't moved, her back to the woman.

Her reaction was drawing attention, too. Those closest to her were beginning to whisper, their eyes shifting back and forth between Letty and the approaching woman.

"It's taken me a while to track you down, daughter. You disappeared so unexpectedly. And changing your name. That was a nice little trick. You might call yourself Letty Stanton now, but you're still Nicolette Stanley in all the ways that matter. How many years has it been, Nicolette, since you walked out on me, your only remaining relative?"

Letty set down the drinks she'd been about to hand to someone. She squared her shoulders before turning to face Mrs. Stanley, but not a single word passed her lips.

Mrs. Stanley reached out as though to hug her daughter, but Letty sidestepped her, giving the woman a wide berth.

Dawson finally snapped out of it and turned to the light-board. He began to flip switches, shutting down the auditorium lights one row at a time. "All right, folks! Time to clear out. We'll see you all for rehearsal tomorrow night."

The group began to disperse, but it was obvious that those

hanging out by the doors hoped to learn more about what was going on. After all, people who dripped wealth and privilege didn't walk into their midst on a daily basis. Never mind that the person in question had called Letty "daughter."

Mrs. Stanley reached for Letty again, but the younger woman flinched and backed away.

The older woman turned her attention to Dawson. "Thank you, Mr. Bauer."

It shouldn't have been possible, but even more color drained from Letty's face. Dawson stared at her, unable to look away. Unwilling to look away and leave her alone in this moment, a moment he never intended to happen — at least not like this. Restoration? Yeah, he'd hoped. Seeing Letty blindsided like this had never been the plan, though.

"It gave me such joy to learn that you'd found my dear Nicolette."

Dawson stood helplessly as Letty put all her walls back in place. Her spine straightened and her eyes turned to ice.

"Letty..." He reached out a hand.

"Oh, dear. How quaint. It's one thing seeing the name on paper, but hearing it? It sounds so... perfectly common, wouldn't you say? Is that what you wanted? To be so ordinary that no one would give you a second glance? I have news for you, Nicolette dear. No one gave you a second glance to begin with. You've always been so dull that you're essentially invisible."

Letty turned her back on her mother and on Dawson and pushed her way through what remained of the dwindling crowd. She rushed toward an out-of-the-way side exit as though a pack of feral wolves were snapping at her heels.

Dawson gave chase. "Letty!"

~

IT WAS two in the morning before Dawson gave up looking for Letty.

He'd tried the coffee shop. Knowing what he did about the kitchen door, he even managed to bust his way into the shop so he could go up and knock on her apartment door. To no avail. Thankfully no police showed up to escort him off the premises.

He'd also stopped by Sally's house, waking her and risking her wrath. Letty wasn't there, either. He'd gone to the church and looked in every window. If he'd known where Philip lived, he'd have gone there, too. Mrs. Butler had answered her phone, listened to his plea for information about Letty's location, and then promptly told him he was a cur before hanging up.

Out of ideas, he'd started driving around town. For hours. Hoping for a glimpse of Letty, for divine intervention, for something to ease the crushing weight in his chest and tell him she was okay.

Dawson parked in the driveway of his rental and climbed from his car. He stood there staring up at the night sky.

"If I was a lesser man, I'd deck you while your attention's elsewhere."

Ah. "Philip."

"I hear you've been harassing the fair citizens of Gilead."

"Not harassing. Just... hoping."

"Hoping for what? To ruin people's lives? You do understand that people don't usually run away unless they have something to run from, right? Or are you a complete imbecile?" If the bite in Philip's words got any sharper, he'd be drawing blood.

Dawson kept his gaze on the sky but watched the older man out of the corner of his eye. "She felt safe with you."

Philip blinked and took a step back. "What kind of nonsense are you up to?"

Dawson finally looked at the man who had rescued Letty all those years ago. "I asked her one time if she was safe when she got here to Gilead and you took her in. I thought you were some creep perving on a young girl."

Philip's fists clenched and his jaw tightened as he stepped closer to Dawson.

"She told me that she was always safe with you. It wasn't the words so much but the way she said it. I got the impression that wherever she'd come from had not been safe."

"And yet you found her mother and dragged that woman here. You're a real prince."

"No. No... Not like... I didn't..." Dawson hung his head and fisted his hands in his hair. "None of this was supposed to happen."

Philip crossed his arms and widened his stance. He wasn't going anywhere. "You'd better start explaining. I'm not too far away from rounding up the townsfolk with pitchforks and torches."

"Can we go inside?" Dawson was bone tired. And Gilead was frost-bite cold.

Philip tipped his head toward the house's front door. "After you."

16

L etty stared at the natural wood beams in the ceiling. A boulder might as well be resting on her chest for all her ability to take a deep breath. She'd been lying in the same position for hours.

The oblivion of sleep had shunned her, and she'd been left to watch the night pass and the new day come with the changing of the shadows on the cabin's ceiling.

Someone stronger might have just gotten out of bed and accepted that she wouldn't be sleeping.

Letty was anything but strong, though.

That woman...

She brought out all of Letty's darkest fears.

She reminded Letty of all the things she hated about herself.

One look at her mother's face, and Letty was again that weak child who'd cowered in fear and covered dark secrets over with lies and fake smiles.

By her presence alone, Letty's mother poured shame out in a burning torrent over her daughter's head.

Letty's chest tightened until her breaths came in short pants, little bursts of air moving in and out of her lungs — but not enough to do her any good. She turned onto her side and curled in on herself as darkness began to creep in around the edges of her vision.

LETTY BLINKED SLUGGISHLY, fighting to get her eyes opened.

A stubborn old man in flannel and denim sat in a chair in the room's corner. "Hey, there."

Panic cleared the cobwebs. "The shop…"

Philip waved her words away. "The girls and Mrs. Butler have you covered for as long as you need."

"How'd you find me?"

Philip's smile was just shy of grim. "When you didn't show up at my place, I figured the hunting cabin would be your next stop."

"Ha. I can't believe you still call it a hunting cabin." Philip wasn't a hunter. It was his escape-from-mankind cabin. He'd loved running that coffee shop, but sometimes the constant flow of people had made him a little crazy, and he'd had to escape. The little rustic cabin in the middle of nowhere had been his answer.

"You okay, kid?"

"Nope." Letty bit the word out.

"Fair enough. You eaten anything?"

"Not hungry."

"Now, there… did I ask if you were hungry?"

"Watch it, old man. You're not the boss of me." The banter should have comforted her, but each word was a lance through her soul. Was she going to have to leave this place? Would everyone hate her now? Her mother had perfected the art of spreading stories to turn everyone against her.

The thought of losing the home she'd grown to love was too much. Letty closed her eyes and hugged her middle.

"I tracked down that boy of yours."

"Boy?"

"Lawson."

The corner of Letty's mouth twitched. "Dawson."

"Whatever."

Letty rolled out of bed to answer nature's call. Not to eat whatever food Philip was going to try to shove down her gullet. Even so, as she sank into a chair at the kitchen table, she didn't reject the coffee the old man pushed her way. The plate of huevos rancheros was another matter, though. She managed to pick up the fork, but before she could take the first bite, her stomach roiled in protest.

She put the fork down and gave the plate a shove. "No can do."

Philip shrugged, dumped the food into the garbage can by the back door, and brought her some plain buttered toast instead. "Try that."

She eyed the toast warily but picked up a piece and took a small bite from the corner. When her stomach didn't do anything too crazy, she chewed and swallowed before trying another small bite.

"So. Lawson..."

She lifted an eyebrow. "Dawson." Why did she bother correcting him? It's not like she was ever going to see or speak to Dawson again. She shouldn't care what Philip called him.

"He spent all last night looking for you. Called Mrs. B at eleven. Showed up at Sally's at midnight."

Letty's heart — the traitor — did a little flip-flop in her chest. "Don't care."

"I had a nice little chat with him around two in the morning."

"Still don't care." Okay. Total lie. She cared. She just didn't want to care.

"He never had any contact with that woman who showed up in town."

"Lies." Petty as it might be, it warmed Letty's heart to hear Philip call her mom *that woman*.

"I'm not gonna tell you everything he said. He needs to explain himself to you. But I'll give you the gist."

"Not interested."

Philip ignored her protests. "He thought he recognized you. Talked to his mom to see if she could think of anyone they might know named Letty. Later, he told his mom to forget about it. As far as he knew, that was the end of it. Either his mom kept asking around, or she'd already asked the wrong person about you."

"You don't know?"

"He hadn't talked to her yet."

She finished off the first piece of toast and washed it down with coffee. "They're tight."

"I'm not joking when I say he spent every single minute of last night looking for you. The fool drove around town for hours. Like he'd see you crossing a street or something."

"Still doesn't add up. They're close. He definitely talked to his mom Sunday night."

Philip shook his head. "I believed him when he said he hadn't. But why does it matter to you?"

Why, indeed? "I don't trust him."

The smile reached all the way to Philip's eyes, giving them a glow that would look just a little bit crazy on anyone else. "You don't trust anyone. Why would Lawson be any different?"

"I trust you."

"Pff. It took you six years to trust me. You've known Lawson for, what, a month?"

She rolled her eyes at the old man before starting on the second piece of toast.

"Letty girl, I need you to listen to me." His voice dropped. Philip wasn't a serious guy. He didn't do heart-to-hearts with people. She'd always figured it was because he didn't want anyone trying to do the same to him.

"What?"

Philip ran a hand down his face before he leaned forward, resting his forearms on the table and clasping his hands together. "After you'd been here about six months, I hired a PI."

Her heart jumped into double-time and the toast fell from her fingers.

He didn't move. He just kept talking in that steady way of his. "I was worried about what you were running from, and I wanted to be prepared in case it showed up here chasing you."

She couldn't hold his gaze. Instead, her eyes kept seeking out the door. Everything in her urged her to escape. To flee. But Philip was right. She did trust him. Hopefully it wouldn't come back to bite her.

"I know about your dad, but the PI couldn't find much about your mom. Nothing substantial, anyway. He got the vibe that things weren't what they appeared, but even your school records didn't reveal much. Stuff was missing. One page would refer to a report, but the report was gone. Stuff like that."

"How did you..." Her words trailed off. How had the PI not tipped off her mom all those years ago? How hadn't she been found?

"I, uh... I had the PI lay some false trails."

Letty stared at the man across the table from her. "Say what?"

Philip held her gaze. "I know it's not the most honest thing to do, but you needed protecting, and you wouldn't tell me what you needed that protection from. So I had the PI lay some false trails to lead people far from Gilead if they ever looked for you. I never figured it was enough to stand up to actual scrutiny. It was just meant to buy a little time, maybe a month or two. Long enough for you to get comfortable and tell me what was going on."

"Months?"

"Yeah, but nobody ever came. Good thing, too, because it took you years to get comfortable around me. A few months wouldn't have done squat to make you trust me."

She wrapped her hands around her coffee mug as she tried to find the words. There was only one to be found, though. "Why?"

"Why'd it take you so long to trust me? Only you can answer that."

"Why'd you go through so much effort for a stranger? I could have been a serial killer. Or a psychopath."

"Give me some credit, kid. I'm not blind now, and I wasn't blind then. You're as much a serial killer as I am the tooth fairy."

She grimaced. That wasn't a mental picture anybody needed. "But why?"

"You know I lost my wife the year before you showed up in town."

Her nod was tight, stiff.

"And we couldn't have kids."

She gave another nod.

"I was still kind of a mess when I got a call about a hungry-looking girl sleeping at the bus depot. Sure, I'd helped people before. This felt, though... I know this is going to sound crazy. But it felt like God was giving me a chance to do something Pauline would have done, to be the kind of person Pauline would have... I don't know. It felt like I could honor her memory and make her proud by being the kind of person you needed in that moment. Defending you against whatever had you running so scared was a natural part of that. I never questioned it. I just did it."

She was dumbfounded. "You took me in. You gave me a place to sleep and food to eat and a path to earn my way in the world. Pauline would be so stinking proud of the man you are, but I'm pretty sure that's the man you were before I came along, too. That's probably part of what she fell in love with."

Philip stared at her through glassy eyes. "I wish you could have known her. She'd have loved you so much."

Letty brushed at the moisture stinging her own eyes. "I don't know what to do. I don't know where to go from here."

"Go?"

"I don't know if I can face her. Face the town. I don't know if I can..."

"You're one of the most stubborn people I've ever met. Which is saying a lot because — well — you've met me. You can do whatever you set your mind to. I've got your back. And — hey — don't sell this town short. Trust the people who have spent the last ten years getting to know you. They're not fools. Except maybe that Lawson. Punk kid."

17

The cowbell clanged as Dawson opened the door to Heavenly Brew. He stepped inside, inhaled the familiar scent, and let his eyes wander the interior.

Four days had passed since that colossal disaster of a Wednesday evening rehearsal. He'd done his best not to stalk Letty, but he'd walked by Heavenly Brew each day and not seen her, and he'd driven by each night and seen no lights in the apartment above. She hadn't been at church, either.

He'd gotten plenty of side-eye from Sally, though. And when Audrey had come over to say hello to him, Sally had taken her daughter's hand and led her away, saying, "We don't speak to strangers or bad men."

Even kindhearted Mrs. Butler had gotten up to move when he'd had the nerve to sit in the same row as her during the worship service.

Dawson doubted it was possible for a man to feel more like a pariah than he did.

He got in line to order, and when he made it to the register, the girl behind the register glared at him, grumbled under her breath as she took his order, and then handed the cup to Cici. "Feel free to spit in it."

Dawson took his hopefully spit-free coffee and moved to the back corner. He didn't dare ask anyone directly where Letty was. He was liable to get a fork to the eye if he did something like that. He could sit and listen to the talk, though. Somebody was bound to say something that would clue him in.

He wasn't even three sips into the best coffee Gilead had to offer when the door opened and Mrs. Stanley breezed in. She demanded some fancy drink with artisan almond milk and freshly grated nutmeg.

Dawson had a pretty good line of sight to Cici. While he saw no saliva touch the order, he did watch a healthy dose of grade A whole cow's milk go into the cup.

Hopefully the woman was lactose intolerant.

Then, of course, because his luck was just that good, Mrs. Stanley walked over to his table. "Dawson, it's so good to see you again. I had such a great time chatting with your mother the other day."

Dawson rolled his shoulders before taking another drink of his coffee.

"I'm so grateful that you helped me find Nicki. I've missed her desperately."

He rose from his seat, took his coffee, and moved to another table.

The woman had the nerve to follow him. Then she stood there, holding her fake fancy coffee, and started talking. Loudly. "You can't imagine how heartbroken I was when Nicki killed her dad. I mean, poor thing, she didn't mean to, I'm sure. It's not like it was... you know... *murder*. But still. She killed her dad and then broke my heart by running away. I looked everywhere for her. Poor thing. I was so worried."

That was it. He was done.

Dawson stood up, faced off with Letty's mother, and let out all the roiling, boiling feelings he'd been holding so tightly inside.

"She ran away from you, Mrs. Stanley. Why do you think that is? What is it about you that made Letty feel she was safer on the streets than in your house? Seriously, what kind of a mom goes out of her way to publicly shame her child with half truths and insinuations? What kind of mom shows up out of nowhere and goes out of her way to try to ruin her daughter's reputation? Her business? Her livelihood? Her friendships? Exactly what kind of a mom are you, Mrs. Stanley?"

Letty's mom glared at him, lips tight and eyes narrowed. "Now, listen here..."

"I'll tell you exactly what kind of a mom does all those things. A bad one. A really freaking bad one." Dawson walked out of the coffee shop, leaving his unfinished coffee behind. What he wouldn't give for a shower. Just being near that woman made him feel like he was covered in grime.

THAT NIGHT, Philip showed up to rehearsal. Dawson silently helped the fifty-something man haul in the food and drinks and get them set up on the tables.

"What? You're not going to ask about her?" Philip's voice held a clear challenge.

"If I do, will you give me a straight answer?"

"Guess you're not man enough to find out, now, are you?"

Dawson started for his sound booth. But what did he have to lose? He turned back around to face Philip. "Is she okay?"

"Okay? That's pretty vague and subjective."

Not that he was prone to violence, but if ever Dawson had felt the urge to cause bodily harm to one of his elders, this was that time. He settled for something that he wouldn't have to apologize for later. "Is. She. Okay?"

Philip grunted and turned his back on Dawson to help someone from wardrobe.

"How's our dear, sweet Letty? I've heard the most awful things about her…" Petra, Mrs. Alleghany's niece, awaited his response with squinty eyes and a sour expression.

Philip's posture went from rigid to cut-from-stone. "Did you want something to eat or drink? Because that's all I'm serving here. If you're in the mood for gossip, you'll need to go somewhere else."

"Oh, well… do you have any kombucha?"

Philip handed the woman an off-brand bottle of green tea. "Here you go. Practically the same thing."

After Petra walked off, Philip stood with his back to Dawson. "She might go to work tomorrow."

The words didn't even register at first.

Who? What?

When it sank in and Dawson realized the gift Philip had given him, he did the only thing he could. "Thank you."

"Don't make me regret it."

DAWSON SAT in his car waiting for the neon *open* sign to light up the window. When it finally did, he got out of the car, pulled his coat tight around him, and hurried across the street.

The cowbell announced his arrival.

The wide eyes, dark circles, and hint of a snarl on Letty's face telegraphed the nature of his reception.

"Please hear me out."

"No."

"Please, Letty."

"No. I've heard you out too many times already."

"Please. Let me explain."

"Look, I don't know what you think this is supposed to be, but relationships shouldn't be this hard. One day, you seem like a great guy, and the next day you ghost me. Then you seem like a great guy, but you betray me to the last person on this planet I ever wanted to see again. I won't play this game with you any more."

"Letty..." She'd thought of them as being in a relationship. Could a word ever give a person so much hope and simultaneously cut him so deeply?

She went about her opening routine, pulling chairs off the tabletops. "You might even be a decent guy. It's possible. But each time I let you get close, I get burned. So, no. Whatever this might have been or could have been is over. It has to be, or I'll end up a smoking husk of charred flesh and bones."

He couldn't help the tiny smile that her words evoked. Such graphic imagery. Such passion buried under a mask of indifference. If she was going to talk over him, though, and cut him off, then he could do the same. Turnabout being fair play and all that.

"When I thought I recognized you, I asked my mom if we knew anyone with your name that was near my age. It was either Chicago or San Francisco. We lived in the Bay area until I was sixteen and we moved to the Windy City. Your name didn't ring any bells with her, though, and I thought it was over. Then I realized on my own who you were. Nicki. I had the wildest crush on you in middle and high school. I finally got up the nerve to ask you to dance at your fifteenth birthday party. And two weeks later, I learned that we were moving to Chicago."

Her movements stuttered for the briefest moment before they picked up again.

"You were always the most beautiful girl I'd ever seen. You

didn't smile often, but when you did, you lit up the whole world. I considered it a privilege just to be on the fringes of your orbit. I probably would have loved you from afar forever had we not moved away."

Letty started straightening the pastries she'd already placed in the display case. She didn't cut him off, though. And she didn't try again to kick him out.

"I didn't realize my mom hadn't dropped it. We were at Sally's house when she called me about you. She'd figured out who you were. I told her to let it go, but the damage was already done. She'd mentioned you — and Gilead — in conversations she'd had with old friends in San Francisco. I didn't realize that, though, until much later. After your mother showed up..."

Letty stiffened.

"Aside from a few hormonally dramatic teenage moments, I'm pretty sure that's the first time I've ever raised my voice to Mom. She's always kind of been my hero. But... you were so hurt, and I was so torn up. Your pain was my fault, and I didn't know what to do with that."

"If your mom's a nice person, you don't blame her for your problems. That's a good start."

His heart tap-danced in his chest. She was speaking. Progress. "Yeah. I think you'd like her."

"I'm allergic to moms."

"You like Sally."

She shook her head. "That's different."

"I knew something was wrong. I knew there was a reason you'd left San Francisco. I didn't know what it was, but I didn't think for a minute that you would have left without good reason. Even in middle school, you weren't impulsive. You were the girl who considered the consequences. If you left, there had to be a reason, and I was pretty sure that reason was related to your mom. I just didn't have the details yet, and I wasn't brave enough to ask you."

"It seems that a lot of people have made it their business to know my business."

"When I asked if you'd ever been to San Francisco, you shut down on me. It took me a week to get you to speak to me again. I was afraid that..."

She slid the display case closed with a bang. Hands on her hips, she swung to face him. "Maybe you're not the worst villain in the world, but in my story, right now, you're still a villain. And I'm not willing to take a chance on you turning out to be anything different than that."

"Letty..."

"Get out. Please. Just leave."

Shoulders stooped, Dawson turned toward the entrance. Not even the sight of Sally and Audrey right inside the door could make him feel any better.

"Is he still a bad man, Mommy? Ah we allowed to talk to him yet?"

"Not yet, sweetie. I'm still deciding if he's bad."

18

Letty's gaze settled on her friend. "You dragged your four-year-old daughter out of bed at six in the morning?"

"Five, actually. It takes forever for this kid to get ready in the morning."

Audrey tugged her hand out of her mom's grasp and raced straight to Letty, holding her arms up for a hug. "I missed you at chu'ch Sunday. Whe' woo you?"

"Well, sweet girl, I needed to get away for a little while. I missed you, though." Letty held the girl close. Such sweet innocence. Dawson was right. Not all moms were bad.

Sally lifted an eyebrow. "Any chance I can get a double-shot mocha? This early rising stuff is for the birds. And crazy people. Maybe crazy bird people."

Letty settled Audrey down in a chair. "What do you say to an egg, bacon, and cheese sandwich?"

The girl pondered. "How about a bacon and cheese sandwich?"

Moving toward the sandwich station, Letty nodded. "Sounds perfect."

"You're going to give my kid high blood pressure."

"But I'm saving her cholesterol."

"With bacon and cheese?"

"Do you want that mocha or not?"

"I dragged myself out of bed at the ridiculous hour of whatever time it is, and you're threatening my caffeine intake?"

"I didn't tell you to get up early."

Sally rolled her eyes. "How else was I supposed to check on you? It's what friends do. Now give me my caffeine."

Letty couldn't help but poke just a little bit. "Or else?"

"You like to live dangerously, don't you?"

Letty sighed, the darkness of her own reality creeping in around the edges of her mind.. "No. Not really. I'd rather live just about any other way in the world than dangerously."

Sally pushed through the little swinging half-door that separated the dining area from the staff area. She walked up to Letty, took the loaf of bread from her hands and put it down, then wrapped her arms around her. "I don't need to know the details, but I need you to know we love you. Audrey and I are on Team Letty no matter what's going on. If that means I need to get a knife and slash Dawson's tires, I'll do it. You just have to promise to bail me out. And make sure to feed and water Audrey until I get sprung from the joint."

Letty lifted her arms and gave Sally a return squeeze. She might have sniffed, too, but if she did, it was just because of Sally's perfume. No other reason at all. "Get out of my way, or you'll never get that mocha."

Sally stepped back. "So, do I need to go knife shopping?"

"He's not a bad guy. Not really. I just... I can't take the risk, you know? There's too much at stake."

"Like what? What's at stake?"

Letty shrugged.

"Ah. Your heart. Got it."

Letty rolled her eyes. "It's not like that."

"Sure. You keep telling yourself that."

Letty tossed the precooked bacon on the grill to warm it before putting it on Audrey's sandwich. "You've got it all wrong."

"Mm-hm. Sure…"

"ALL RIGHT, everybody! Give me your attention." Letty clapped her hands. The three people in front of her stared blankly. Okay, so yeah, she'd already had their attention. They weren't the usual chatty crowd that she needed to rein in.

"Today I'm going to walk you through the concession stand, show you the equipment, and give you the general lay of the land. I only have an hour with you, so that's probably as far as we'll get. Tomorrow when we meet, I'll start showing you how to use the equipment to make the different items we'll be making."

A college-aged boy raised his hand.

"Yes, Marco?"

"You know today's Valentine's Day, right? I mean, some of us have plans…"

Preston snorted and muttered under his breath. "It's an hour. Not the rest of your life."

Letty ignored the second comment and replied to the first. "Today's training has been on the calendar since the start of the semester. If you're just now realizing February fourteenth is Valentine's Day, I can't help you with that. Opening night is next week, and we need to run like a well-oiled machine."

Color stained the kid's cheeks, and Letty felt a moment of pity. Just a moment, though. They had all known the training schedule before they even signed up to be on the concession team. "All right, everyone. Follow me."

She unlocked the door and stepped up into the concession

stand. It wasn't like the little wheeled trailer some colleges and high schools used. This was a commercial-grade concession stand. Once everybody was in the door, she started pointing things out. "This is the hot dog griller. It's kind of like a flat rotisserie that rotates so the dog is evenly cooked all around. Next to it is the popcorn popper. We make buttered popcorn in here, but then we add a sweetened syrup to some of the popcorn and toss it to make a kettle corn that sells well, too."

Letty continued walking through, directing their attention to the cotton candy machine, then the warmer for the pretzels. "Unfortunately, we can't make those fresh. Pretzels are notoriously difficult. So we buy them frozen and warm them here."

"Do we salt them?" Marco, the Valentine lover boy, eyed the pretzel warmer with hungry eyes.

"Uh, yeah. We salt some, put garlic parm on some, and do a cinnamon sugar mix on the others. We leave a few plain." Letty moved on to the cheese pumps. "One for the pretzel cheese and another for nacho cheese."

"What's the difference?" Marco again. Somebody should have eaten his lunch before coming to training.

"Nacho cheese is spicy. Pretzel cheese is not. Some places chintz out and serve nacho cheese with their pretzels, but we don't roll like that here at GBC."

The boy's eyebrows climbed his forehead. "Oh-kay."

Letty turned her back and rolled her eyes. She might not be at her most patient today. It wasn't Marco's fault. "In the deep fryers we do funnel cake, French fries, cheese sticks — mozzarella and cheddar — and corndogs."

"Is that safe? What if we get burned?" This came from the reed-thin girl with big glasses and a worried frown.

"No problem, Janie. That's what training's for. By the time opening night gets here, you'll be able to safely operate every piece of equipment in the concession stand."

"But... what if I don't feel like I can do it safely?"

"Then I'll assign you to a different station. Normally everyone rotates between all the stations so that nobody gets bored, but if you feel you absolutely can't do the deep fryer, no worries. I'll work around it."

The girl nodded and the lines in her forehead smoothed.

"We also do snow cones and have a limited ice cream selection."

Her third helper, Preston, wasn't a student. He was a school donor that Wendy from the Development Office had asked her to put to work. Letty hadn't asked, but she was pretty sure this was the guy Dawson said he knew from Chicago. His eyes assessed the interior of the concession stand before coming back to rest on her. "This seems like a ton of food. It's just a concession stand, but it's like you're serving every food that can be found at the state fair."

"You're not far off. Sadly, we don't have deep-fried pickles or deep-fried green beans. Man, what I wouldn't give for some fried green beans right about now..." Letty shook her head and gave her attention back to the group in front of her.

Marco was rubbing his stomach. He must like deep-fried green beans, too.

"We serve thousands of people here, not to mention those who are working on the play itself. We're not some rinky-dink little concession stand. People come from all over the country to see this Easter play. While the story of Christ's death and resurrection is the focal point of everything we do here, we offer the complete package, and having well-planned concessions is just one little piece of our bigger purpose. The overall impression that GBC makes during the Easter play helps to attract donors, too, that allow us to continue to minister to people through this production. We all have a part to play."

"Some are for honorable use and some for dishonorable use." Preston said it almost to himself, but Letty caught it.

"Exactly. When you look at that passage, you'll see that it's about the body of Christ, right? Each part of the body has a purpose, and not all purposes are glamorous. That's true for the passion play, too. We're not all going to be stars on the stage, but we all have a role, and if any of us fall down on the job, the whole body — the play and the people it ministers to — suffers as a result. So we do our job, and we do it well. In doing that, we serve our brothers and sisters in Christ."

Enthusiasm started to flow into her ragtag team of volunteers. She'd definitely been off her game if she'd forgotten to give them the whole get-fired-up speech to start with. Oh, well. God was working it all out.

"Okay, now, moving on." She showed them another display case. "This is where we put all the candy."

"What about fruit? Or anything healthy? I mean, I know it's a concession stand and fried food is king, but...?" Preston again. What on earth did the man do for a living? He seemed to have a lot of opinions about food service.

She waved a hand. "Yeah, yeah, yeah. It doesn't sell as well, but we do that, too. We bring in some prepackaged hummus with pita chips, different types of nuts, and fresh fruit. We do things like apples and bananas, but we also prepare our own fruit cups that have pineapple, melon, grapes, cherries, or whatever we can get that's relatively kinda sorta in-season somewhere." There was a whole system that went into how many miles they were willing to truck the fruit, but nobody would be interested in that much detail. She wouldn't have been, either, if it hadn't helped her with her own buying-local — or localish — business model for Heavenly Brew.

The team exited the concession stand just as the college's marching band passed by on their way either to or from class. In the chaos of people and instruments and noise, Letty didn't immediately notice the voice.

"Nicolette, dear. Nicolette, how can you treat me like this? You ignore my calls, refuse to speak to me. Your own mother."

If Letty didn't know better — which she did — she might have believed that the teary emotion in the woman's voice were real.

"You're breaking my heart, dear."

Funny how her mother had only sought her out in public places. She did her best work when she had an enthralled audience.

The marching band stuttered to a stop as Letty turned to face her mother. She still didn't have any words. She'd never learned how to defend herself against anything that woman said or did. From the time she was little, obedience and respect for her elders had been instilled in her. Maybe that was part of the reason she'd never stood up for herself. The rest of it, though? Fear. Shame.

So many confused feelings. For years she'd thought it was all her fault. She was to blame for the fact that her mother didn't love her. She was the problem, not her mother.

It wasn't until she'd been in Gilead a few years that she realized how wrong she'd been. Philip had dragged her to church each Sunday, a condition of her living above the coffee shop. She'd hated it at first. Church, however, was where she first came to realize what love was supposed to look like. It wasn't until she'd met the Savior who loved her unconditionally and beyond her wildest dreams that she'd been able to see her mom in a clearer light.

Letty wasn't at fault for her mother's callous and vindictive behavior. She knew that now. She knew it with absolute certainty.

But still... she stood there frozen. No words came to her.

"You know I've only ever loved you..."

The marching band began to shuffle their feet. Their eyes landed everywhere except on Letty. Even her concession team took a step back.

"What did I do that made you leave? If you'd just tell me, I'd apologize. I'd tell you how sorry I am and how much I love you."

Letty stared at her feet for a moment before turning her back on her mother and looking at her concession team. "Tomorrow we'll start learning how to use the different equipment. Come prepared to learn."

Janie avoided her gaze. Marco looked at her like he was inspecting an insect, and Preston's stare was full of inscrutable intensity.

Great. If her team walked out on her, she was going to be in real trouble.

19

Dawson was taking a shortcut through the auditorium's lobby when he noticed the marching band stumbling around like a wild animal had just torn through their formation.

It didn't take long for Mrs. Stanley's voice to reach him.

"If you'd just let me, I'd apologize."

Nope. Not having it. Not today. Letty might not want anything to do with him, but that didn't mean he was going to stand by and let this woman get away with trying to publicly shame her daughter.

"Mrs. Stanley!" He demanded her attention as he pushed his way through the marching band.

She was still speaking at Letty by the time he got within reaching distance.

Putting more steel in his voice, he tried again. "Mrs. Stanley, this is private property, and you need to leave."

The woman cast a glance his way, not quite able to hide the venom in her eyes. "Excuse me?"

"This is a private college, and that makes it private property. You need to leave."

"Oh, Dawson, dear, I think you've misunderstood."

"No misunderstanding here. You're harassing someone who does have a right to be here, and you do not have a right to be here, so you need to leave." Hopefully he wasn't stretching the truth beyond reasonable recognition. Surely the college would side with him.

The venom disappeared, and triumph glinted in its place. "You misunderstand. I'm now a donor, a supporter of this quaint Easter production your little school puts on. I have every right to be here."

Dawson glanced toward Letty, but she was already pushing her way through people to get to the exit. Good enough. The least he could do was keep Mrs. Stanley distracted so Letty could make a clean getaway. "Donor or not, you don't have the right to harass people on campus. And you're not allowed to wander campus without an escort. Security protocols are in place for a reason. How about I walk you to the main office so you can talk to them and get an escort, someone who can give you a proper tour of the campus?"

He wasn't really asking her. There was no way he was letting Mrs. Stanley leave his sight until she was under the control of an official college representative.

As for her being a donor? That was... not good.

He wished he'd never recognized Letty, never asked his mom, never opened this ugly rotting can of worms. He still didn't even understand what was spilling out of the can. He knew it was hurting Letty, though, and that caused him way more pain than he wanted to admit.

Dawson stood outside the door to Human Resources. Mr. Watersby and he hadn't exactly gotten off to an auspicious start, but he didn't know who else to turn to. This was the man who'd told him Letty always saw more than people realized. Which meant he saw her more than she realized. He was an ally... of sorts. Hopefully.

He pushed open the door and nodded to the administrative assistant. "Is Mr. Watersby available?"

She gave him a genuine smile. "He's been expecting you, Mr. Bauer. Go right in."

Expecting him? This wasn't the first time the older man seemed to know more than he should — whatever that was about. He couldn't waste time pondering it, though. So Dawson gave the closed door a single knock before opening it. "Mr. Watersby?"

The older man nodded to him. "Come right in, young Mr. Bauer. What can I do for you?"

Dawson glanced around the office. And at the other faces staring back at him.

Is this what Alice had felt like when she jumped down the rabbit hole?

"Philip." He gave the man a nod. He reached a hand out to one of the other men. "Dawson Bauer. Nice to meet you."

The man was probably around Philip's age but with sun-ripened skin that made him look older. "Larry Groening. Pleasure's mine."

Dawson turned and introduced himself to the last man in the room.

The man's grip was firm as they shook hands. "Rob Matthews."

He was probably supposed to know who these men were, but he hadn't been in Gilead long enough yet to have sorted out all the ways people were connected to each other. Dawson gave his attention back to the man behind the desk.

Mr. Watersby waved an age-speckled hand to the one remaining chair. "Have a seat."

Dawson sank into the chair, feeling a bit like he was about to be interrogated. "I, uh, came to ask for your help."

"It's about time. You've been fumbling around like a three-legged foal." Mr. Groening gave him the kind of stare his father leveled at him whenever he'd done something to disappoint the man.

"Crashing into everything in his path and tripping over his own stinking feet." Philip's stare was less fatherly and had a slight tinge of murder to it.

"What can you expect from a city boy?" Mr. Matthews' sage nod was offset by the twinkle in his eyes.

"Now, now. He's just a kid. What can we expect?" It said a lot that the man who forced him to keep a position he didn't want at the beginning of the semester was the kindest face in the room.

"I, uh..."

"Out with it." The head of HR wasn't going to beat around any bushes.

"Mrs. Stanley was on-campus. I told her it was private property and she had to leave. She was making a scene and harassing Letty."

Philip jumped up from his seat. "Where?"

"I tried to kick her off the campus, but she said she's a donor for the play and has every right to be here. So I took her to the front office and told her she couldn't be on-campus without an escort. Thankfully security backed me up. They said she needed an escort until her official permission is cleared."

Philip started pacing in the back of the room. "That woman..."

Mr. Groening crossed his arms. "What's her game?"

Dawson kept his eyes on Mr. Watersby. "She keeps showing

up wherever Letty goes. The campus needs to be safe. I can't keep Mrs. Stanley out of Heavenly Brew..."

Philip growled. "But I can."

Dawson gave the man a quick nod before returning his attention to the head of HR. "There has to be a way to keep her off campus. Why did the college accept a donation from her? Can we give it back? If I can find someone to take her place, to donate in her place, can the college reject her donation and revoke her right to be on campus?"

Mr. Watersby tented his hands and tapped his fingers together. "Let me see how sizeable a donation we're talking about. Then I'll see what I can do. Do you honestly have someone who can donate in her place?"

Dawson nodded. He'd beg his parents if he had to. "Yes. Probably. If it's not too much."

Philip grunted behind him. "How much is too much?"

Mr. Groening leaned forward in his seat. "The amount shouldn't matter if the integrity of the college is at stake."

Mr. Watersby nodded to the other men, ignoring Dawson. "I'll get some answers."

Mr. Groening stood and placed his hat on his head. "I'll leave you to it. I have places to be. Let me know if I can help. Otherwise, I'll see you all at poker night."

Mr. Matthews also stood. "I should go, too. I need to pick up Wren."

As soon as he slipped out the door, Philip turned to Dawson and pointed a finger at him. "You said it was an accident. You said you were going to talk to Letty and fix it."

Dawson hung his head. "I tried. She won't speak to me. She listened a little bit... and then she kicked me out."

"So help me, if she gets hurt even worse than she already has..."

Dawson jumped to his feet. "I'm not here to hurt her. I'm trying to protect her. I'm trying to help."

Philip grunted again before looking at Mr. Watersby. "You haven't been wrong yet, but so help me, if you're wrong about this one—" He hooked a thumb in Dawson's direction. "—I'll hold a grudge the likes of which you've never seen."

Laughter twinkled in Mr. Watersby's eyes. "Of course, Philip. I would expect nothing less."

The moment Philip left the office, the older man looked at Dawson. "Do you plan to give up on her?"

"Of course not." Could the man be any more insulting?

"Good. She deserves someone who's willing to fight for her, you know."

He nodded. "I know. And I will. Fight, I mean."

"You seem to have fallen awfully hard in a short period of time."

Had he? Yeah, he had. He wasn't ready to label what he felt, but still... "Whether she ever wants anything to do with me again or not, Letty deserves to know that she matters, that people see her and care for her and want her to be okay. I think she's spent most of her life hiding, and as a result, she thinks she's invisible. She thinks that nobody sees. That nobody cares."

Mr. Watersby nodded. "I'll see what I can find out about the donation."

Dawson turned for the door.

"And Mr. Bauer?"

He paused.

"I'd say your assessment of Letty is sound. She *thinks* she's invisible, but she's not, is she?"

Dawson turned back. "She couldn't hide if she tried. She burns far too brightly for that."

"Indeed." The man nodded before reaching for his phone. "Now have a nice day."

20

Thank goodness Valentine's Day was in the rearview. If one more person had waxed poetic about romance and love and Cupid, she might've actually decked them. The holiday itself was bad enough, but on the day after, every single stinking person who came into the shop had to ask her what she'd done for Valentine's Day. Or, worse, tell her all about whatever romantic thing they'd done the night before.

You'd think people would have something better to talk about.

She was half-tempted to bring up politics just to get people fighting mad so she didn't have to listen to all their gooey-eyed happy love stories.

"Are you still making the sweetheart special?"

Letty returned her attention to the customer at the front of the line. "Ah... no?"

Mrs. Plugh pouted. "It's so good, though. White chocolate raspberry mocha. What better drink in all of creation could there be?"

"Um... you could just order a white chocolate raspberry

mocha. The drink can still be made without the Valentine's name."

The woman crossed her arms and tapped her toe. "Are you telling me, Letty, that you can't humor me by writing 'Sweetheart Special' on my cup?"

She looked down at the Sharpie sitting next to the register. Could she do it? Could she write that gimmicky romantic name on the cup without being tempted to jump across the counter and run out the front door screaming at the top of her lungs?

Mrs. Plugh leaned over the counter. "You look like I've asked you to stab a puppy in the eye. Now who's being dramatic?"

Letty took a deep breath and labeled the cup the way Mrs. Plugh wanted before accepting the woman's cash and making change.

Mr. Abrams sidled up to the register next. "Just plain ol' coffee for me, dear. No romance necessary."

She reached for his favorite coffee mug when he whispered. "I heard she auditioned for Mary, the mother of Jesus, this year. Did you see it?"

Letty tried to hide her smile and gave one of her favorite customers a nod.

"As dramatic as ever?"

She gave him another nod. "Like you wouldn't believe."

The retiree chuckled. "I'm half convinced she does that each year just to get all the newbies to loosen up and have a good time with their auditions."

He might have a point there. "I guess, all things considered, it's better than handing out shots to all the folks waiting to audition."

Mr. Abrams' eyes crinkled with mirth. "Bite your tongue, dear. People are way too uptight about a little alcohol now and then."

Letty handed the coffee mug over before lifting her hands in surrender. "I'm not touching that one with a ten-foot pole. You'll have to fight that battle on your own."

He took his cup, twirled his cane, then headed over to where she had the coffee carafes all set out in order from lightest roast to darkest.

When she turned back to the customer line, Letty let out a sigh. "Hi, Mrs. Alleghany. What'll it be today?"

In a stage whisper not even remotely meant to be quiet, the woman said, "How is everything going with your long-lost mother, dear?"

"For here or to go?"

"I've heard some disturbing things around town about you since your mother has shown up. If there's anything you need to talk about, you know I'm here for you."

Like a buzzard waiting to pick the flesh from a carcass. That kind of *here for you*. "Just coffee today, Mrs. Alleghany? Or something else?"

The woman scowled at her. "Just coffee. For here."

Great. She'd be sticking around. Letty processed the payment, then handed Mrs. Alleghany one of the paper to-go cups.

"But I said for here."

"You never know when you might get called away. Better to be prepared." She could always pull the fire alarm if she had to.

A group of actors from the play were next. "Hey, Connor. What can I get for you?"

"Just coffee. And maybe... do you have any chocolate cream pie?"

"Not today, but I have peanut butter pie."

He wrinkled his nose. "What's that?"

"It's like Reese's Pieces, but in pie form."

"Sure, I'll give it a try."

She rang him up while Cici plated his pie.

The last of the college group gave her a strange look as she took his order. "Anything else?"

He shook his head. "I'm in the marching band. I was there when your mom showed up."

If a person could get an Olympic gold medal for teeth grinding, Letty would definitely be in the running.

The kid scuffled his shoes on the floor. "She said some kind of awful stuff about you."

As if she didn't know that. "I sell coffee. Not conversation."

His eyes widened before he nodded and backed away, taking his coffee cup with him.

Mrs. Callaghan stood there next. She might have been a soft-spoken and gentle soul, but she'd also tried to fix Letty up with Dawson when he'd first shown up in town. "Do you have any carrot cake today?"

"No carrot, but I have apple raisin cake with cream cheese whipped cream."

"Cream cheese whipped cream?" The woman squinted her eyes.

Letty held onto her patience. "It's like cream cheese frosting, but lighter. Not so heavy or super sweet."

The woman held her gaze for longer than strictly necessary. "Okay. I trust your judgment."

It was a weird choice of words, and Letty would take some time to think about it later, but for now she was just trying to survive the furtive glances from everyone in the dining room. It felt like every single person there was talking about her, about her mother, or about her relationship with her mother. Non-relationship, really. Non-mother, too, for that matter.

LETTY KEPT LOOKING over her shoulder when she arrived for another day of concession stand training. She wasn't sure there was a safe place left in the world. If she didn't have Heavenly Brew, she would have seriously thought about leaving Gilead. Maybe. She had Sally and Audrey. And Philip.

It wouldn't do any good to run away, though. Without access to Philip's private investigator — something she wouldn't ask for because she already owed that man way more than she had a right to — she wouldn't be able to cover her tracks. Her past would find her no matter where she went.

So, looking over her shoulder was the best she could do for now. And hope that people didn't decide she was a patricidal murderer and start egging her car or boycotting her business.

Letty's breath caught in her throat. Where had that thought even come from? She massaged her sternum, applying as much pressure as she could tolerate. She couldn't think of her dad without pain blooming behind her breastbone. The stress of her mom showing up, though, had the pain pulsing with every heartbeat.

It took her a minute to realize she wasn't alone. Her team stood there waiting for her, eyes wide as they watched her. Hopefully they didn't realize how close to a meltdown she was. "All right, folks. Today we're going to learn how to make cotton candy and snow cones. The snow cones are pretty easy. Cotton candy's a little trickier, but it's not hard. First, I'll explain the process. Then I'll show you. Then you'll each do it yourselves to get familiar with it."

Marco lifted a hand.

"This isn't grade school, Marco. You don't have to raise your hand."

"Um... if we only have this little bit of experience, how will we be able to handle opening night?"

Letty resisted the urge to groan. There was always one.

"Opening night is next Wednesday. We'll be running the full concession stand on Monday and Tuesday during rehearsal. Think of it as our own little dress rehearsal. Also, for the record, it was on the schedule you received when you first signed up to help. Like Valentine's Day was on that schedule. Did you look at that schedule, Marco?"

The boy's ears turned bright red.

Great. It was official. She was a monster. "Sorry. That was uncalled-for. It's been a rough few days. It's not your fault I'm in a bad mood."

Ears still red, Marco dipped his chin. "Sure."

He didn't sound very sure, but she couldn't dwell on it. Maybe if she tried to be extra nice for the rest of the day, he wouldn't walk out on her before opening night. She could always hope, anyway.

"Um..." He stared at her like he wasn't sure it was safe to speak. Great.

"Go ahead, Marco. What's on your mind?"

"Why does the Easter play start in February? I don't get it. Easter's not 'til April, right?"

Fair enough. "Opening night is always Ash Wednesday, and the final show is on Good Friday. Except for Ash Wednesday, all the other showings are on Fridays and Saturdays. Is this your first year here?"

There went those ears again. Bright red little beacons on the sides of his head. She almost missed his mumbled answer of, "I just never paid attention before."

Huh. Apparently Dawson wasn't the only person in the world who'd managed not to realize what a big deal Easter was at Gilead Bible College.

～

"GREAT JOB, Janie! You're a cotton candy master." She'd even gotten artistic and tried to create cotton candy animals. Some of them had even been recognizable.

The younger woman blushed, but her smile was bright. "It's kind of fun."

They'd managed to learn the snow cone machine, the cotton candy machine, and even the filling and cleaning of the cheese sauce pumps. The latter was everyone's favorite task. Not.

All in all, it was good, as far as one-hour training sessions went.

Letty was ushering her team out of the concession stand when they all came to a stop right in front of her.

Great. The last thing she needed was...

"Letty, may I have a word?"

She pushed through her team. "Mr. Watersby?"

He nodded. "That would appear to be my name, yes."

What did the head of college HR want with her? Was she being fired from a job that didn't even pay her? "Um, yeah. Sure. Give me a second."

Marco and Janie looked at Mr. Watersby like he might sprout another head. Meanwhile, Preston and the older man exchanged a look. She couldn't decipher it, but it was... something.

"Is this guy cool?" Marco never took his eyes off Mr. Watersby as he asked the hushed question.

Oh, dear. Had everyone always been this suspicious, or was her paranoia rubbing off on people? Letty gave her team a nod. "Everything's fine here. Mr. Watersby is a family friend. Or, well, my Gilead family anyway. I'll see you all tomorrow."

The frown lines were back on Janie's forehead as she started backing toward the exit.

The head of HR gave her team a regal nod that seemed to

put them at ease. They eventually all made it through the door, leaving her alone with one of Philip's oldest friends.

"What can I do for you, Mr. W?"

"I've told you to call me Charlie how many times now?"

"Mm. This feels like some kind of official visit."

Mr. Watersby nodded. "Indeed. Care to walk with me? These old bones don't like it when I stand still for too long."

She gave him a nod, double-checked that the concession stand was locked up tight, and accompanied him toward a side door that exited out onto a grassy incline. "It's a little cold out here for old bones, too, don't you think?"

He chuckled. "Maybe. But this is the fastest way to the cafeteria and the hot cocoa they have."

"Heavenly Brew makes a mean cup of hot cocoa, too."

"No argument there."

They walked in silence for a few minutes before she couldn't take it anymore. "What's this about?"

Never one to be rushed, Mr. Watersby walked a few more steps before he replied. "Someone raised concerns about your mother's presence on campus. I did some checking. She made a donation to the fund for the Easter play."

Her heart dropped like a rock. Was her mom going to force them to let Letty go? Why else would Human Resources be involved?

"Gilead's a pretty tight community, wouldn't you agree?" He lifted an eyebrow as he glanced sideways at her.

"If you mean everybody's up in everybody else's business, then yeah. We're tight."

His dry chuckle was so familiar it almost made her ache. "The person in the fundraising office the day your mother made her donation was filling in for Wendy. And shouldn't have been. Wendy was out of the office, and this other person took it upon herself to step in. Apparently she thinks Wendy is overrated and that anybody can do her job. You don't need to know who it is, but rest assured, she has an appointment with me next week."

Letty knew exactly who it was. She and Wendy might not be BFFs, but they were friendly — friendly enough that Letty had listened to a rant or two about Lissa... who was basically a receptionist, if she remembered correctly. She kept that to herself, though, and focused on the rest of what Mr. Watersby had said. "I don't understand. How would things be different if it'd been Wendy who handled it?"

"We vet our donors. We don't want someone who also donates to a military regime that promotes genocide to be financially supporting the work we do here for God."

"My mother isn't exactly genocidal." Probably.

He tugged her hand through his arm and rested it on the crook of his elbow. "Of course not, dear. But she still should have been vetted."

"Would it have made a difference?"

"That's neither here nor there. Someone offered to replace her donation in order to have her removed as a donor."

Letty's steps faltered. "What?"

"Two somebodies, really. One person offered to make a donation to take the place of your mother's if the school would cut ties with her. Then somebody else offered to match the initial amount — basically doubling the gift — if, again, the college would cut ties with her and block her from future donations."

Her feet started moving again, but her knees were barely holding her up. "Who?"

Mr. Watersby shook his head. "It was all quite anonymous."

"That's... I don't know what to say."

"Of course, it's only been forty-eight hours since your mother showed up on campus claiming to be a donor. Word hasn't really gotten around yet, not by Gilead standards. So the eight hundred or so other smaller donations that have come in, all with notes demanding that GBC not allow Mrs. Stanley to be a donor, are probably all just the tip of the iceberg."

Shock froze Letty in place. Again. "Eight hundred?"

He nodded. "From the community at large. I dare say, before today's over, the initial donation might well be tripled. Who knows what we'll see by the week's end. Rather extraordinary, really."

"Eight hundred?"

"How was it you put it? Everybody's up in everybody else's business?"

"Eight? Hundred?"

He tugged her farther down the path. "Like I said, Gilead is a tight community."

"But everybody's been acting so strange around me. Ignoring the whole thing as though..." She let out a soul-deep sigh. "They believe everything my mother's been spewing, and they hate me."

"Are you quite so sure about that? It seems that you may have decided what people think without bothering to ask them. And that your reasoning may have a fatal flaw."

"It's not flawed. Everyone always believes my mother. It's been that way my whole life." She wouldn't mention the times she'd gone to a teacher or even the school administrator for help only to be told she shouldn't lie about her mother.

He patted her hand. "Maybe back where you came from. This is Gilead, though. Remember? When everybody's in your business, that means that everybody knows you."

"But..."

"They know you, Letty. Give this town a chance. Don't judge us based on your previous experiences. Besides those two large donations, eight hundred other people sent in whatever money they could scrounge up to try to replace your mother's donation.

They didn't do that because they had to. They didn't do it because they had money to burn. They did it because they know you, and because here in Gilead, we look out for our own. And you're one of ours."

"One of…"

"One of ours."

Was that true? Did she belong in Gilead? She'd worked hard to blend into the background.

"We see you, Letty Stanton. We see your heart. We always have."

"But…"

"Shush and let me buy you a hot cocoa. It might not be as good as you can make, but it's always been the company that makes a drink worth the time and money. That's why Heavenly Brew's done so well since you came on board."

She gave Mr. Watersby her best side-eye. "You're Philip's friend. Aren't you being a tad disloyal?"

His smile was broad. "Even Philip would tell you that he's a cantankerous old fool on the best of days. People never stopped in to drink his coffee because they loved his company or because his smile brightened their day. They stopped in for coffee because it was cheap and the other people drinking there were worth the time. Then you came along. You made Heavenly Brew a place people went out of their way to visit. *You* did that. Nobody else. You. Letty Stanton."

Letty's steps faltered. She'd never felt quite so exposed. And yet… warmth pervaded her heart. Gilead saw her. And Gilead — or at least eight hundred of its residents — loved her.

She nodded to Mr. Watersby. "Okay. Cafeteria hot cocoa sounds good."

21

D awson sat in Sunday school waiting — hoping — for Letty to walk through the doors. She didn't, of course. Not that he could blame her. If he was the reason she was staying away, though, then he could find another class. Another church. He wasn't going to rob her of the people who loved her just because he wanted to be one of those people, too.

Whoa.

Say what?

Did he want to... love... her?

He'd known her, what, maybe six weeks?

That puppy love torch he'd carried for her all those years ago might've burned brightly, fueled by all those teenage hormones. But it didn't really count.

So, yeah, six weeks.

That was too fast for the L-word.

Right?

It wasn't like he was in love with her. He just wanted to be one of the people who was in her corner and on her side and cheering her on as she went through life. He wanted her happiness. He wanted to see her overflowing with happiness.

That wasn't love.

His phone vibrated in its holder as class was letting out. He made his way into the sanctuary before pulling it out.

His mom. Everything okay?

No. But what could he say? How could he explain it all? As okay as can be expected.

She didn't reply, and he didn't have the energy to be worried about her silence.

Audrey turned and waved at him from three rows up. He smiled and waved back. Maybe one of these days Sally would decide he wasn't a bad man and Audrey would be allowed to talk to him again.

Dawson's eyes scanned left to the girl's mom and then left again to...

"Jesus came t' Sunday school!" Audrey's attempt at whispering to him alerted not just her mom but also half of the sanctuary.

Sally bowed her head a moment before saying something in the girl's ear.

Audrey shrugged, threw another wave his way, then turned around to face forward.

Letty. She was in church.

He sighed his relief.

If he also took a few deep breaths to ease the ache in his chest, nobody needed to know that.

After all, it wasn't like he was in love or anything.

Dawson sat in his seat as the service ended.

He always enjoyed a good sermon, but he'd been in church a lot of years. It wasn't often that he heard a sermon that really made him think. He got convicted on a regular basis, sure. But to be hit by a sermon so hard that he had to stop and take a hard look at his life? That hadn't happened in a long time.

He needed to sit for a minute, though, and reflect. It had been that kind of message.

He felt rather than saw someone sink into the pew behind him.

So much for solitude.

"Good sermon."

Dawson twisted in his seat to nod, but the sight of Mr. Abrams' earnest eyes caused him to turn more fully. "Yeah. It was."

The older man — one of Letty's favorite customers — gave him a nod. "'The Lord is near to the brokenhearted and saves the crushed in spirit.' Psalm 34:18 is one of my favorite verses. I don't think I've ever heard a sermon on it before, though."

"What makes it a favorite of yours?"

"You don't live to be my age without experiencing a few broken hearts, without burying a few loved ones, without seeing people you care about making destructive choices, without experiencing the pain of betrayal a time or two. No, sir. You don't live to be my age without understanding all the way to your bones what it means to be crushed in spirit."

Dawson knew it was prying, but... "When did you first find this verse helpful?"

Mr. Abrams lifted his cane an inch or two off the sanctuary's wheat-colored carpet and tapped it back down. He repeated the motion a few times before he answered. "My oldest boy was career military. Loved his job. Died in service to his country. It broke my heart, sure enough. Watching my late wife's heart break, too, though? That was worse. So, so much worse."

He shouldn't have asked. Mr. Abrams was right. You didn't get to be his age without having walked some hard, hard roads.

The older man cleared his throat before continuing. "God

was with me, though. I survived because of Him. Someone wrote this verse in a condolence card they sent. I don't remember who sent it, but the verse burned its way into my consciousness. I took it as a promise of God. He was near. He would save me from the pain. And He did. He has every time since, too."

"Sometimes it's hard for people to let go of their pain, though." Like Letty. She seemed to be holding onto her pain with a death grip.

Mr. Abrams winked at him. "That's because we're fools."

Dawson chuckled. "I'm not sure the person I'm thinking of would appreciate being called a fool."

"Sometimes our pain feels like armor. We hold it close to us because we think it's somehow protecting us from more hurt." He tapped his cane on the floor a couple more times.

Dawson mulled over the older man's words before speaking. "But how do I help somebody if that's what they're doing?"

Mr. Abrams stared at him with keen eyes surrounded by age-marked skin. Silence stretched between them until Mr. Abrams gave a nod, seemingly satisfied with whatever he'd seen on Dawson's face. "You can't force a person's heart to change. All you can do is give them opportunities to think right and to choose right. You can't force a person's heart to look at the world — or at you — a certain way. But you can give them opportunities. And you can love them enough to let them make choices other than the ones you want. You can love them enough to let them choose a path that doesn't include you if they believe that's where God is leading them."

"I didn't mean... I wasn't talking about..." Romance. He wasn't talking about romance. Mostly not, anyway.

The older man's eyes twinkled. "A long time ago, a wounded bird landed in the town of Gilead. Those who bothered to look could see that her wings were broken. We had no idea what kind of wild animal had wounded her so gravely, but we patched her up the best we could. We knew the day might come when she would take her healed wings and fly far away from the town that had invested so much of itself into helping her get well again. The bird, though, was so used to being wounded that she never quite seemed to realize her wings had healed. She never tried to leave, but she also never chose to stay. She just existed from day to day, not even realizing she had a choice."

The older man who always seemed to take such joy in flirting with Letty stood. He shuffled his way into the aisle and toward the exit, leaving Dawson to stew in his thoughts.

What was it Mr. Watersby had said? That Letty wasn't as invisible as she thought she was.

Dawson turned back around to face the front of the now-empty sanctuary.

He needed some time.

God, help me to let her go. If it's Your will, please help me to let her go. But more than that, Lord, please help Letty to see how loved she is. Help her to recognize that she has a choice.

22

L etty pasted a big smile on her face as she nodded to her team. "We'll run the full concession at rehearsal for the next two nights to help us get into fighting shape for opening night on Wednesday. Is everyone ready?"

Marco scuffed his shoes against the stamped concrete floor. "Sure."

Janie took a boxing stance on the balls of her feet. "We've got this."

Preston couldn't have looked more bored if he'd tried, but he gave her a nod that seemed almost friendly.

"All right. If you have any questions, don't wait for me to guess that you have one. Holler for me, and I'll come to you as quickly as I can." With that, she unlocked the door to the concession stand, flipped on the power breakers, and moved into the space that felt like a second home after Heavenly Brew — at least during play season.

"Hey, boss, what do I...?" Marco stared at the hotdog griller like the secrets of the time-space continuum were hidden between its little rolling warmers.

"The switch is on the back. Flip it on, then get the hotdogs out. They're on the top shelf in the freezer."

Janie got to work setting up the pretzel warmer and filling the cheese pumps while Preston pulled a block of ice from the freezer for the snow cone machine.

Letty filled the deep fryer with fresh oil and set the gauge so it could start getting up to temperature. Thank goodness Preston'd had the bright idea to move the snow cone machine farther away from the fryer. With all the times she'd battled melting ice, you'd think she'd have thought of that herself, but oh, no. It took Wendy's pet project from Chicago to shine a light on the fatal flaw of having the snow cone machine right next to the deep fryer. Added bonus, Janie could now man the snow cone and cotton candy machines together.

With the candy display cases set into place on the counter and the sign with prices hung and ready to go, Letty took a step back to admire her team's work. The first night they ran the full concession was always hit or miss. The team was still gelling, and they hadn't committed all the tasks to muscle memory yet. This was a good group, though. They'd do well together.

"Boss! What about the corn dogs?" Marco was staring at the hotdog warmer where he'd also placed the corndogs. "They don't look right."

Letty shook her head. "They need to be deep fried first. They don't go onto the warmer 'til they've come out of the deep fryer."

"Oh, yeah." Marco's ears pinked up as he pulled the corn-dogs back off the warmer and carried them over to the not-yet-hot deep fryer. "Um. What do I do...?"

Preston grabbed the deep fryer basket off the back. "Here. I'll cook them once the oil's ready."

"Right, right. Thanks, man." Marco shuffled back to his station.

"Don't worry about it, Marco. First night jitters. Happens to the best of us." Letty gave the young man a smile. This time she even kind of meant it.

His shoulders relaxed, and he gave her a nod. "No problem here, boss."

When had he started calling her boss? She wasn't sure, but she kind of liked it. That kind of power could go to a girl's head if she let it.

"Hey, Letty!" The familiar voice sounded from outside the concession stand.

"Jess, hey there. How's your costume readiness tonight?"

The girl rolled her eyes. "Dress rehearsal starts in thirty. And those disciples..." She brought her fingers to her lips, gave them a kiss, and then released them into the air. "I've got the best job in the whole play."

Letty tried not to laugh at the girl's boy-crazy enthusiasm. Had she ever been like that? No, not really. It was nice to see someone whose biggest problems appeared to be deciding which of the disciples was the cutest in a robe, though. There was a kind of innocence to that. Hopefully nothing ever came along to rob Jess of that innocence.

"Go get 'em, tiger. But, you know, maybe no claws. I hear they're murder on costumes." Letty waved Jess on, and the younger girl threw her another grin before darting away toward the auditorium.

Letty let her eyes roam the lobby. Most of the crew was already where they needed to be, so she wasn't likely to see...

Oh.

There he was.

Dawson poked a head out of the auditorium doors and looked right at her. When he stepped out the rest of the way, she had the urge to crouch down on the floor and let somebody else help him. But that would look foolish, even if hiding from

Dawson was actually the smart thing to do. He made her feel all kinds of unbalanced.

He jogged over. "Got any kombucha tonight?"

The question was directed at Letty, but when she didn't answer right away, Janie jumped in. "We sure do. What flavor would you like? We have candied apple, cotton candy, grape-fruit, and hot ginger. That one burns a little on the way down, but it sure does taste good."

Dawson's eyes stayed on Letty as he answered the younger girl. "Candied apple, please. I hear it's a huge hit with the younger crowd."

Janie got his bottled beverage. "Can I get you anything else? Nachos, a soft pretzel, some candy?"

That girl was going to be queen at upselling.

Dawson shook his head. "Not right now, but I'm sure I'll be out again later. What do I owe you?"

Janie cast a wide-eyed look at Letty. "Employee discount?"

Letty gave the girl a nod. "Thirty percent off for cast and crew. Dawson is crew."

The girl rang the order up, and Dawson swept his card in front of the reader device. Before she knew it, he was jogging back to the auditorium with a bottle of candied apple kombucha in his hand.

"I think there's something wrong with the drink machine." Marco's voice pulled Letty's attention away from the auditorium doors.

"What is that?"

Holding the cup out to her, he said, "It's supposed to be Pepsi, but..."

"Either the syrup's not hooked up correctly or it's running on empty." Letty got to work checking on the boxes of syrup for the soda dispenser. Just another busy shift in the concession stand for Gilead's Easter play.

LETTY LIFTED another chair from the tables and set it on the floor The play would have its opening show when evening came, but until then, she still had a business to run.

Just another sleepy Wednesday morning in Gilead, Kansas.

Until an elegant woman walked in the door at Heavenly Brew.

Definitely not a local. Letty knew all the locals, and none of them dressed like Jackie O.

"I'm told you have the best coffee in town. Do you recommend anything specific?"

Letty blinked at her. "Coffee?"

The woman's laugh sounded of bells warmed by the summer sun. "I gathered. Any specific drink you can tempt me with, though? What's your specialty?"

Letty shook her head. "Sorry. I've been up for hours, but I'm apparently not conversation-awake yet. I have a pomegranate dark chocolate mocha today. I'm kind of trying it out. I saw these dried pomegranate seeds that were dipped in dark chocolate. They were delicious, and I wanted to try it out as a drink. It passed my taste test, but I haven't gotten any customer feedback yet. You'd be the first. Everything else on the menu is pretty standard except for the marshmallow mocha that's always popular around Easter."

"Only around Easter? That seems a little odd."

Letty shrugged. "I think it's all the commercials about marshmallow candies that come out this time of year."

The woman nodded. "I guess that makes sense. Adults want the same candy that kids eat, but they need it to feel more sophisticated."

"I suppose we all like to feel adult even when we're acting like kids."

The woman agreed with a flutter of her hand. "Indeed. Your pomegranate mocha intrigues me — I'll try that. You must have quite a sense of adventure to try out new flavors like this. Do your customers enjoy trying them, too?"

Letty rang up the woman's drink. "For the most part. Some folks don't like to try new things. I have one older guy who's in here every day ordering a hot mocha. If I tried to get him to drink anything else, he'd probably revolt on me. In general, though, I think people like to have a little adventure in their lives. They don't want it to feel like a risk, but they like a little taste of it. If someone decides they hate a new concoction I've made, I'll replace it with a drink of their choice. That makes me — and my coffee — a pretty safe bet. And it makes people feel important when I ask for their feedback about a new flavor. That's important in customer service. People want to feel like they have a voice and that their voice matters."

"Hm. There's wisdom in your words, and I think it applies to more than just customer service. You have good insight into human nature."

Letty moved toward the espresso machine. "Nah. I'm just good at observing people."

The woman's smile was warm as she took her drink from Letty. She sipped before nodding. "I think this one's a keeper. It was a pleasure to meet you, Letty." Then she took her drink and stepped back out into the cold.

Several minutes passed before Letty realized the woman had called her by name even though she'd never introduced herself.

Who on earth...?

The thought wasn't fully formed yet when a group of high schoolers charged through the door to get their morning fix before school started.

The fancy lady with the nice smile was all but forgotten as the morning rush got into full swing.

23

The house lights were up, and the stage was dark with the curtain drawn. The show would be starting shortly, and Dawson had a detailed — sometimes minute-by-minute — agenda of what needed to be happening with the sound and the lights at each step of the way.

He'd passed by the petting zoo out in the parking lot on his way in. He'd never thought of a passion play as being a place where people would tailgate, but the groups of people already congregating in the auditorium's parking lot told him differently. It might not quite match the professional sports level of tailgating, but then when had Gilead ever copied somebody else? Gilead and her residents marched to the beat of their very own drum.

How he'd ever managed to sign an employment contract with Gilead Bible College without knowing about its Easter play was wild. Everyone in the Northern hemisphere knew about this play, yet he'd been blind to it.

Thank goodness, too.

If he had known about the play, he'd never have taken the job. Maybe, in some ways, Letty would have been better off if he hadn't burst onto the scene. In other ways, though... He couldn't imagine what his life would be like if he hadn't met Letty. Despite the trouble he'd brought into *her* life, he couldn't be sorry he'd run into her again. She might not be the same girl he'd known all those years ago, but she was still extraordinary, and he was beyond blessed to know her.

"Are you ready for this, young man?"

Dawson turned at Mr. Watersby's voice. "As ready as I can be."

"Any regrets?"

Was he reading Dawson's mind? "Regrets?"

"I know it was hard for you to work on an Easter play."

Oh... *Oh.* "Gilead's been good for me."

"Just Gilead? Or a certain young coffee entrepreneur?"

Heat warmed Dawson's face. Great. He was blushing. What was it with this town and interfering wise old men?

Mr. Watersby nodded, having the grace to ignore Dawson's obvious discomfort. "I know we got off to a rocky start, but from the moment your application came through, I knew you were the right man for this job. I knew Gilead could help you just as much as you could help Gilead."

Dawson gave the older man his full attention. "How did you know?"

Mr. Watersby shrugged. "Discernment. A whisper of wisdom from God. Something like that."

"Any regrets about hiring me? I've brought my share of drama to Gilead."

The older man's eyes brightened. "Easter is such a special time, isn't it? It reminds us of Christ's sacrifice, but also of his resurrection. It reminds us that when this world has made something dead — whether it's a heart, a hope, or a relationship — God can breathe new life into it. Regrets? Not a single one. You're not done here in Gilead, and she's not done with you."

She... as in Gilead? Or Letty? "I'm not sure what you mean."

"Time will tell, my dear boy. Time will tell."

Mr. Watersby gave his cane a little twirl before moving up the aisle of the auditorium. The audience wasn't allowed in yet, but in Dawson's experience, the head of HR rarely got turned down, let alone turned away.

When this world has made something dead, God can breathe new life into it.

Is that what had happened to him? He hadn't been dead-dead, but inside? He'd shut down in so many ways. He'd scorned Easter, of all things. He'd told himself it wasn't so bad because he wasn't turning his back on his Savior. He hadn't walked away from his faith... but he'd stopped walking in the fulness of it, in the fulness of Christ.

Sunday's sermon came back to him in a rush. He'd been so sure it was about Letty, about her brokenness, about her crushed spirit, but... How arrogant could he be? He hadn't even realized that the sermon was as much for him as it was for her, as it was for anyone else. He'd been so willing to deflect by pointing the finger elsewhere — even with the best of intentions — that he'd been blind to his own need for healing. God was near. In the pain, in the heartache. God was near with arms open and ready to offer comfort and solace.

Dawson closed his eyes and bowed his head. *I'm sorry. For all of it. Maybe if I'd just gotten angry and yelled it out, I would have gotten over it sooner. We'll never know. But I'm sorry I let distance grow between us, and I thank You for never letting me go, for never letting the distance get too big. You pursued me everywhere I went, and You brought me here to Gilead. Thank you.*

When he opened his eyes, people had begun filing into the auditorium.

Show time was almost upon them, and he'd lost the only

chance he would get to run out to the concession stand and see Letty.

As much as he'd wanted to see her, though, he'd needed to hear what Mr. Watersby had said. He'd needed that time with God, too.

"AFTER-PARTY FOR CAST and crew at the GBC Cafeteria!" One of the Roman soldiers passed the word, his cape swishing behind him as he went.

"You coming?" Jess, the wardrobe girl who was moonlighting at Heavenly Brew, asked as she passed by.

"Uhm... not sure." Hanging out with a bunch of college kids high on the adrenaline of a good opening night didn't quite fit Dawson's idea of a good time.

"You should totally come." The girl bounced up onto her tiptoes. "I hear Letty's going to be there."

Dawson's gaze snapped to Jess's.

She gave him a cheeky grin. "Come on. You know you want to come."

Maybe a cafeteria party wasn't such a bad idea after all...

DAWSON FOUND himself surrounded by what felt like most of the town of Gilead.

Good grief.

Just how many people could be crammed into a cafeteria, anyway? It was easy to forget just how many people it took to put on a full-scale production until all those people showed up at the same time.

He'd never find Letty in the midst of this crush.

"Hey, you're Dawson, right?"

He looked to the woman standing with Preston. She'd been with Preston when they'd run into each other at the grocery store, too. At the time, he'd thought she had sad eyes. They didn't seem so sad anymore. Earnest, yes. Maybe even kind of cautious. But lighter, too. "Yeah. That's me."

"I'm Wendy. I'm in charge of fundraising here at GBC. I'm really sorry about what transpired with Letty's mom. I wasn't in the office that day, or that never would have happened. We have procedures and protocols." She grimaced. "Anyway. I just wanted to thank you for bringing it to Mr. Watersby's attention and for all you did to help rectify it."

Dawson reached his hand out, shaking hers. "No need to thank me. I know it can't have been easy to face that woman and tell her you were returning her money. I appreciate everything you did to help Letty, too."

Wendy gave him a quick nod. "It's always a good day when doing my job and doing right by a friend go hand in hand like that."

Preston was watching Wendy as though the sun rose and set in her eyes. Dawson wasn't exactly a romantic guy, but he'd be shocked if there wasn't something going on between the two of them.

They moved off into the crowd, and Dawson continued his semi-methodical scan of the place as he tried to find Letty. Before he got far with his search, though, someone tugged at his arm. He looked down to see Jess standing there.

"See? I told you she'd be here." Then she shoved Letty at him before ducking away into the press of people.

"I'm firing her. First chance I get, she's gone. As soon as I find someone else who's dependable and will work Saturdays." Color stained Letty's cheeks as her gaze studiously followed the younger girl rather than meet his.

"And your chances of finding a good Saturday employee?"

She finally glanced his way. "Mrs. B's been great."

"She's not exactly going to be doing your heavy lifting for you."

Letty fidgeted with the ends of her hair. "No, I suppose not. I guess I'll be keeping Jess on for the foreseeable future."

"Sorry—"

"Sorry—"

Dawson stopped himself from talking over her. "Can I go first?"

She gave a single nod, and he maneuvered them out of the thick of the crowd. "I didn't mean any harm when I asked my mom if she could think of anyone we knew with your name. I'm still sorry, though. My simple question has led to a lot of grief for you. It hurts me to know that you're hurting, and if there was any way I could take your hurt away, I would."

Letty picked at her fingernails for a minute before speaking. "I know you didn't mean anything by it. I'm sorry I cut you off like I did and wouldn't let you explain. I was drowning in so much hurt that I couldn't figure out exactly where it was coming from or who was behind it. So I struck out at anyone brave enough to come within striking distance."

Dawson chuckled. "Does that mean you're calling me brave?"

She shrugged, but the corner of her mouth lifted. "Don't let it go to your head."

"Has anyone ever told you that you're extraordinarily brave yourself?"

The color that had finally faded rushed back into her cheeks. "Not hardly. When life got hard, I ran away."

"You might look at the past and think you ran away from something hard. I look at it, and I see what you ran toward. You ran toward a life full of challenges but also full of joy. You ran toward a life where you had a chance at meeting people who would love, support, encourage, and care for you."

Her voice came out whisper-soft. "I ran toward a life with Christ. I didn't know it at the time, but God guided my steps the whole way. He took me from a place of so much pain and brought me to a place where I could learn about His Son. If I hadn't run, I might've never come to know Christ, and I can't imagine what my life would be like without Him."

Dawson rested a finger under Letty's chin and gently tipped her gaze up to meet his. "I know you went through some really hard things, and I hope someday you'll trust me enough to share some of them with me. Know this, though, Letty Stanton. I'm glad you ran away and had the chance to grow into the beautiful woman you've become."

24

L etty let herself into Philip's house as quietly as she could. It was close to midnight, and Philip had promised to open the coffee shop for her in the morning. It would be pretty poor form on her part to wake him up only hours before he was going to have to rise to get the baking started.

"I'm beginning to wonder if I went too easy on you when you were a teenager. Maybe I should have been a little more heavy-handed with the whole curfew thing."

She jumped. "What are you doing up?"

"Waiting for you."

Letty rolled her eyes before joining Philip at the kitchen table. "You should be sleeping."

He shrugged.

"You were worried."

Another shrug. "The play ended hours ago."

Letty chuckled before getting up to fill the kettle. "Hot cocoa sound okay?"

Philip grunted.

"There was an after-party at the cafeteria. Jess dragged me there."

"That girl is something else."

"Yeah. Then she shoved me at Dawson and disappeared."

Philip lifted an eyebrow.

Letty scooped the cocoa mix into two mugs while the kettle heated. "We talked."

"You and Jess?"

"Don't be dense, old man."

His chuckle warmed her. "I'm thinking about picking up a shift or two each week."

Huh? That came out of nowhere. "At Heavenly Brew?"

He snorted. "Where else? The firehouse?"

The kettle started to hiss, and Letty unplugged it before pouring the water into the two mugs. "How come?"

"Retirement's getting kind of boring. And I miss your charming personality."

She handed him his cocoa. "Opening shifts?"

"Do I look desperate?"

He could try to come across as grouchy as much as he liked, but she knew his heart was made of marshmallow goo. "Desperate for a friend, maybe."

"This is the thanks I get. Just great." The twinkle in his eyes belayed the words.

Letty sipped her still-too-hot cocoa. "Thanks for letting me bunk here."

The famous Philip shrug made another appearance. "I get it. I wouldn't want to stay above the shop with that viper still running around town."

A smile pulled up on her lips. "Viper, huh? Pretty strong words there, old man."

"So, you and Dawson talked?"

She choked on her cocoa and coughed. "Way to... change... the... subject."

Philip toasted her with his mug. "Did you guys kiss and make up?"

"Um... no kissing. But I apologized."

"Mighty big of you."

She took a more tentative sip of her cocoa this time. "I've been a jerk to him. You know that."

"I wasn't denying it. Just didn't realize you'd figured it out, too."

Letty leaned back in her seat and met Philip's gaze. "Thank you."

He tilted his head to the side, the question in his eyes.

"You gave me a safe place to live. You helped me legally change my name when I turned eighteen. You dug up my past and instead of harassing me about it, you helped to protect me from it. You..."

"I did what any decent person would do. I'm not anything special."

Letty grinned at the man who had given her the opportunity to thrive in life when she'd been too afraid to even hope for survival. "You did what any grouchy, argumentative, cantankerous, decent person would do."

Color tinted Philip's cheeks as he concentrated on the mug of cocoa in front of him.

Letty rose from her seat, walked around the table, gave him an awkward side hug, and kissed the top of his head. "Thank you."

Then she climbed the stairs to the spare room. She'd been crashing in it since Philip had found her hiding out at his hunting cabin.

Philip had... he'd been the hands and feet of Jesus that she'd so desperately needed in her life.

He'd given her a safe place to sleep, given her a job, made sure she ate. Yeah, he'd done all of that. But he'd also dragged her to church with him — a condition of living above the coffee shop. She'd sat there, sullen, angry, and terrified, through so many of those church services. She'd lost count. Eventually, though, she'd accepted that she was probably safe. She'd realized that Philip was exactly who he'd appeared to be. Not perfect. With a big bark. But real and sincere and good. And seeing that in him had given her the freedom to start to actually listen in church, which had ultimately led her to the Cross.

That man was solid gold.

A tap at the bedroom door drew her attention. He didn't open it, but instead spoke through the wood. "You might not know it, but you saved me, too. I'm not sure I could have gotten through the grief without you. God knew exactly what He was doing when He brought us together, and I'm thankful every day for it."

Footsteps padded down the hall and away from her door.

Yep. Solid gold.

Maybe she should suggest to Jess that Philip would be a good subject for her matchmaking attempts...

LETTY WALKED into Heavenly Brew at the crazy time of ten o'clock in the morning.

It. Was. Glorious.

She needed to work on finding a reliable opener. Someone she could trust not just to show up on time, but also someone she could trust to do the baking. Someone she could trust with her recipes. She needed more balance in her life, and hiring someone to open would be a good first step.

A quick second after the joy of walking in at ten o'clock

flowed over her skin like a nice, bright breeze, the noise of the morning hit her.

Her eyes took in the dining room. Heavenly Brew did a decent business, and some mornings it was downright brisk. This morning, though? They were packed.

Every seat was taken, and people were scattered in standing clusters throughout the dining room.

In all her years in Gilead, Heavenly Brew had never been this full.

She darted behind the front counter. "What can I do to help?"

"Bring out baked goods!" Philip shouted over the din.

A line of cups waited for Cici to make the drinks, but Philip was right. The display case was nearly empty. She hustled into the kitchen only to find Dawson elbow-deep in soapy water and Mrs. B dropping off a filled tray from bussing the tables.

"Hello, dear. I just came in for coffee this morning, but it's a good thing. You need all the help you can get with that crowd out there." The older woman gave Letty a sunny smile before sweeping past her, cleaning cloth in one hand and empty tray in the other.

Dawson gave her a nod as he scrubbed away at the breakfast dishes. "I had the morning off work and was hoping to see you. Philip seemed happy for my offer of help, though. Which speaks to just how desperate he was..."

Letty threw a grin his way before reaching for the closest baking rack. "Thanks for the help!"

She made several trips back and forth as she filled the display case with more breakfast pastries. Even the cookies and brownies had run low, and they didn't usually start to move until lunch.

When she was done with that, she jumped into the drink line to help Cici. At one point, she looked out into the dining room to soak in the joy of a bustling coffee shop. The woman from the day before —— the one who'd made her think of Jackie O — was there. She was dressed more casually today. Slacks, blouse, stylish sweater with an overcoat draped over the back of her chair. A man was with her. A man she... recognized.

From somewhere.

How did she know him?

He was in his sixties? Maybe older.

White hair askew. Little half-glasses pushed up on his head.

Familiar... but also not.

Letty shook the unsettling feeling away. She hadn't seen her mother for a while, but having her lurking around town and popping up at random and inconvenient intervals was making her jumpy. Not every stranger in her shop was a threat from her past.

She forced herself to concentrate on the drink order in front of her.

Hot Chai Latte xtra Chai and a DATE with Letty wink wink

Yes, Philip had written out "wink wink" on the cup.

She glanced over at the register, caught the scowl on Philip's face and the laughter in Dawson's eyes, and shook her head as she went to work on his drink.

The noise level had dropped, but not by much.

While the cafeteria party the night before had been for cast and crew, everyone who attended the play wanted to have a place to talk and debrief and discuss what had changed from the previous year, how the actors had done, whether the right shade of pink had been used in the sunrise scene. Everything. The play was so much a part of Gilead that the townspeople cared about every aspect of it, whether they took part in the production or sat among the audience.

Everyone had an opinion, and sometimes they weren't so favorable. Even so, almost every opinion came from a place of care. Gilead cared. Sometimes the care came across as overbearing, nosy, and meddling. Somewhere along the way, Gilead's way of caring had sunk into Letty's bones. She'd gotten comfortable with it. She even kind of expected it.

She called out the order just like she always did. "Hot chai latte, xtra Chai, and a date with Letty. Wink, wink."

"Woohoo!" Mr. Abrams cheered from his table. "Now you're talking! Can I get what he's having?"

"Remember when Alberta's nephew proposed to Henrietta's daughter?" Mrs. Butler's voice was softer than most, but everyone heard and offered their assent.

Even people who hadn't been in Heavenly Brew that day knew the story of how Alberta's nephew had bribed Letty to put his marriage proposal on the cup and then call it out as part of the drink order. He'd been so wildly in love. And so painfully shy.

Mr. Abrams — with not a softspoken bone in his body — yelled across to Mrs. Butler. "And now they have a happy marriage and three young'uns. Not a bad romance record for a coffeeshop."

Dawson took his drink. "Is that a yes?"

She shrugged. "I suppose."

His smile was modest, but his eyes danced. Then he glanced at the dining room, and his smile faltered. "I... uh... need to do something. Then I'll get back at the dishes."

Huh. His attitude had turned on a dime. What was that all about? "Sure. No problem."

Dawson approached the table with the fancy lady and the almost-sort-of-familiar man. His shoulders were tense and his posture stiff.

She would have kept staring if Philip hadn't shoved a cup into her hand. "Help Cici. We're falling behind on drink orders."

25

Dawson stared down at the woman who oozed elegance out of every pore. "What are you doing here?"

"I wanted to make things right."

"By showing up unannounced?"

She didn't so much as flinch. "I stopped in for coffee yesterday. Your Letty seems like a lovely woman."

His Letty. He liked the sound of that. But... "Yesterday? What did you say to her? She's going to think I set her up, that I knew and didn't tell her."

"We just chatted about coffee. Give me some credit, dear. The last thing I want to do is sabotage your love life. I'd like to have grandchildren someday, after all." She lifted a refined eyebrow at him.

Dawson hung his head. "I love you, Mom, but Letty does not handle surprises well."

"It's understandable. She hasn't had very many good ones, from what I gather."

He tipped his head to the man at the table but kept his eyes on his mom. "Who's this?"

His mom winced. "I might not have thought this through very well."

Dawson put his chai latte down, crossed his arms, and did his best to channel his dad's take-no-prisoners glare. He'd never been able to withstand that look as a kid.

The man held out his hand. "Eric Carlisle. It's a pleasure to meet you, Mr. Bauer."

He couldn't ignore the man, especially not with his mother right there. So he shook Mr. Carlisle's hand. Then he again looked at his mother. "Who is he?"

Color stained his mom's cheeks. This was most definitely not going to be good if it had Mom blushing. "He's the executor of Mr. Stanley's will."

"Mr. Stanley? As in Letty's dad? That Mr. Stanley?"

She nodded.

Dawson closed his eyes, took a deep breath, counted to eight, and released the breath. He'd have counted higher if he wasn't worried about passing out and leaving Letty unprotected. "You both have to leave."

Mr. Carlisle's eyes widened. "I need to speak with Miss Stanton."

Dawson's mom reached across the table and patted the man's hand. "Of course you do, and you will, but my son is correct. Showing up like this was not a good choice. It wasn't a kind choice. We need to do right by this young woman, and blind-siding her is not going to engender her trust."

Mr. Carlisle frowned even as he nodded. "Very well. I'll return to my hotel. My flight leaves in the morning, though. If we don't have this settled before then, we'll need to schedule another time."

Mom's smile was gracious. "Of course. I'll keep you posted."

Dawson sank into the man's vacated chair and reached for his own drink. The woman sitting across from him had always been kindness personified. Elegance, too. But today she was pale, her eyes were shadowed, and she'd almost forced her way into Letty's life in a way that was anything but graceful. "What's going on, Mom?"

She blinked before tucking a stray lock of hair behind her ear. "I felt terrible about stirring all this up and leading that woman to Letty. I wanted to help. So I did some digging. You know your dad and Letty's dad used to be in a prayer group together?"

He leaned back in his chair. "Seriously?"

She nodded. "You should ask your dad about it. Maybe it's something Letty would like to know someday, too. They knew each other fairly well, as it turns out."

"That still doesn't explain Mr. Carlisle."

Mom swirled the coffee in the bottom of her cup before setting it down and pushing it away. "I did some digging, and that led me to Mr. Carlisle. He was Mr. Stanley's attorney, the executor of the will, and he's in charge of Letty's trust."

She had a trust fund. That was... something he'd have to think about later. It made sense. But he didn't have the energy to ponder the implications at the moment. "So you decided to drag the poor man to Gilead, Kansas?"

His mom gave a tired smile. "I learned some things. Like rumors about how Letty's dad really died. And some things from your dad about trouble in the home and steps Mr. Stanley was taking to protect Letty, and... I poked around asking all these questions, and because of that, I reintroduced a horrible human being into Letty's life, and I just wanted to make up for it. Mr. Carlisle has a letter that Letty's dad left for her. She would want that, right?"

Dawson slammed back the rest of his latte to buy some time. "Yeah, she would. But not here. Not in public. Not like this."

Mom nodded her head. "I know. I don't know what I was thinking. I just..."

"You were hurting for her."

She nodded. "Your dad told me this was a bad idea."

"And you ignored him?" That was saying something. His folks were nearly one hundred percent in sync with each other about the important stuff.

"And look where it got me. A parental lecture from my son." A small smile tugged at the corner of her mouth.

"You know I love you, right? And it's not your fault. None of this is your fault. We all played a role in bringing Mrs. Stanley to Gilead, but the blame for the ugliness in her relationship with her daughter rests on her shoulders and hers alone. Not yours. Not mine. Not Letty's."

She reached over and rested her hand on his. "You're a good man, Dawson Bauer. You must have wonderful parents who raised you well."

Dawson threw his head back and laughed. When his laughter eventually died down, he glanced up and caught Letty staring at him and his mom, a frown on her face. He winked at her before rising from his seat, giving his mom a kiss on the cheek, and returning to the kitchen.

26

Letty took the tray of dirty dishes from Mrs. Butler before the older woman could protest. Then she used her hip to swing open the door into the kitchen area. She carried the dirty dishes to the correct side of the sink, offloaded them, and stared at Dawson.

"Can I help you with something?" The words were to the point, but his voice held humor.

"Who was that woman?"

"What woman?"

She growled at him. "You know what woman. The one with the shiny hair and fancy clothes. The one who looks like she's never accidentally stumbled into a wall even once in her entire life."

Dawson peeked up at her from where he stood, stooped over a sink full of soapy water. "Can we talk later? I'll tell you who she was and what she was doing here."

"Am I going to be upset about it?"

He pulled a hand out of the suds and wriggled it back and forth. "Maybe. Maybe not. You would have been upset if I'd introduced you to her and her companion in front of a full restaurant, though."

She took a step back. "Did you know she was coming?"

His head shook emphatically. "No. Which is why I told them to leave. It wasn't fair springing that on you."

Every fiber in her being told her to turn and run. But she wanted to know... "Who is she?"

He gave her his full attention, looking at her with soft eyes. "My mom."

Letty sputtered. "Your... your mom? She was in here yesterday! I met your mom and didn't know it!? I don't even know what I was wearing. I was probably covered in flour and lard. Oh, good grief."

Dawson's smile stalled her rant. "She felt bad for the way everything happened and how your mom showed back up in your life. So she did some digging. She found your dad's attorney. He's the executor of your dad's will. He has business with you."

Letty's gaze swung to the mercifully closed kitchen doors. "And they just waltzed in here with that?"

He dried his hands on a nearby towel before reaching out and tucking a stray lock of hair behind her ear. "Which is why I told them to leave. When you're ready to have that meeting, we'll get it scheduled. No rush. No pressure."

"Okay. Um... okay."

"Any time."

She turned and started for the door. Before she pushed through, though, she stopped and turned back to Dawson. "Thank you for having my back."

A grin split his face. "Any time."

Liking a man who was kind and thoughtful and who put her needs first was easy. A little too easy if the fluttering in her chest was any indication. That could wait for later, though. The time would come when she needed to figure out how she really felt about him... and if that was how she *wanted* to feel.

Was she making things harder than they needed to be? Part of her was sure something inside of her was fundamentally broken. Her ability to love only went so far, so deep. Was she making an unconscious choice to barricade her heart? Or was she simply not capable of lasting love? Of a real adult relationship?

AFTER THE SHOP closed for the day, Letty sat at one of the tables in the back. She enjoyed the quiet and was rather fond of the shadows, too. This place had been her sanctuary for such a long time that its very walls were steeped in peace.

Well... as long as *that woman* stayed away.

Her phone dinged with a text from Sally. LET ME IN.

She glanced up from the screen to see her friend lurking outside the front door.

Not a moment's peace. Gilead at its finest.

Letty let Sally in before returning to her seat in the back corner.

"What on earth are you doing in here sitting in the dark?"

"I needed to think about some things, but I got interrupted." She gave Sally a faux glare.

Her friend laughed. "I ran into Dawson at the grocery store. He seemed... contemplative."

"Where's Audrey?"

"I see what you're doing there. I say something about the good-looking guy who has a crush on you, and you say something about my adorable and mischievous daughter. Is that how this whole conversation is going to go?"

Letty shrugged. "I'll have you know, Audrey's one of my favorite topics of conversation."

Sally couldn't keep her laughter in any longer. "My daughter is at the ice cream shop with your good-looking guy. Because I wanted to check on you, and I didn't want little ears listening."

Whoa. Sally didn't let Audrey spend time with just anyone. "I guess that means he's no longer a bad man?"

"He's... on probation."

Letty grinned. "He might be on probation with me, too."

"I heard he asked you out on a date via chai latte."

"Gilead rumor mill?"

"Audrey told me."

Wow. The rumor mill had stepped up its game. "Your daughter was already in school when it happened. How on earth did the news make it to her?"

"You know Suzie Smith? She's in Audrey's preschool class."

Letty lifted an eyebrow. "We don't exactly socialize..."

Sally cut her off. "Philip told Larry who told Mr. Watersby, but Mr.Watersby's assistant overheard them, and her sister is Suzie Smith's mom."

Letty snorted. "Yeah. Makes perfect sense. I can totally see it."

Sally rolled her eyes. "Suzie's mom helped out in class today. Grading papers or something."

"Preschoolers have papers that need grading?"

Sally shrugged. "Just go with it. It's what I do."

Letty shook her head, and the two sat in silence for a bit before she finally said what was on her mind. "Did you listen to the sermon this past Sunday?"

"Yep. It was a pretty good one. I think it applied to a lot of people, too."

"In what way?"

"Some people hold onto past hurts in the form of unforgiveness, and that's never good. Some people hold onto past hurts by turning them into anger against God. Some of us weaponize our hurts and use them to bludgeon anyone who tries to get close to us. I think it's something we all struggle with — but in different ways, you know?"

She nodded. "That makes sense. How do you handle your past hurts?"

"I used to hold onto them good and tight. It was turning me into a bitter old woman before my time, too. I had to learn to trust God's sovereignty, to trust that He knew what He was doing even if I couldn't see a way through the mess. I had to let go of the hurts and let go of the pain if I truly wanted to have joy in my life."

"How... How did you do that?"

"I wanted Audrey to have a good mom. I wanted her to someday have good memories of growing up. So I had to let it all go and kind of leap headfirst into the joy of the Lord. If that makes sense." Sally shrugged as though what she'd just said hadn't been profound.

Letty nodded again. "Perfect sense. I don't have an Audrey, though."

"But you have a *you*. Do you want to be someone who looks back and sees only darkness hovering over her life, or do you want to look back and see light?"

"Light and dark. You make it sound so simple."

Sally grunted. "Not simple, no. Not always easy, either. But real. I can't help but think you've spent a decade here in Gilead, and yet you've never really set down roots. You've never really allowed yourself to start living."

"I own half a coffee shop!"

"Yeah, you do. But you still sleep in a room above it. Or a room at Philip's. And you could have bought out the rest of Heavenly Brew. You know Philip would have financed you. But you didn't want to. You said you wanted to buy it outright, but part of me always wondered if it was because you wanted to be able to walk away at some point if things got too hard."

Heat burned in Letty's chest. "You think so little of me?"

Sally stood from her seat. She scooted around the table and hugged Letty from behind. "I love you. You're one of my favorite people in the world. But you have to admit it — you don't let people in. You have this barbed wire fence built all around you, and none of us can get through it. I always figured that someday you'd whip out the wire cutters and tear that fence down. I'm still waiting, though."

"This is my home."

Sally squeezed her even tighter. "You know everything about everybody in this town because you care enough to listen. But you've never let yourself trust any of us enough to share the deepest parts of yourself. Until your mom waltzed in here, we all assumed your parents were dead or that you were a foster care runaway or something like that. You're the best listener in the world, but you do a lousy job of talking about yourself."

It hurt to hear it, but it was true. Letty reached up and squeezed Sally's arms. "You might have a point."

Sally kissed the top of her head before she moved away toward the front door. "I need to go rescue a man from a sticky preschooler. I'll be up later if you want to talk."

How many times had Sally said that to her over the years? And not once had she ever taken her up on the offer...

27

The last couple of weeks had flown. Dawson had managed not to blow up any stage lights or speakers — always a plus in his field — and the cast and crew had knocked it out of the park at every single showing.

And — did he dare put it into words? He had started — just the tiniest bit — looking forward to Easter.

Letty sat across from him. The unseasonably warm day allowed them to enjoy a date at the park.

He'd kept the dates casual. Low-key. Two of their dates had even been at Heavenly Brew.

She was so tentative that he half-expected her to turn him down each time he asked her out. Every time that woman smiled at him, though, his heart leapt into his throat, and he was filled with hope.

Something about that woman…

"Are you even listening?" Letty's eyebrow was inching northward as she leaned back on the bench, arms crossed.

Dawson blinked and brought his attention back into focus. "Mmm. And thinking about how beautiful your smile is."

Her eyes widened, and color rushed into her cheeks. "You can't keep saying stuff like that."

"Why not? It's true."

She shook her head. "I don't know what to do when you say those kinds of things."

"Don't say anything, then. Just smile. That's enough for me."

"You're exasperating."

"In a good way, though, right?" He lifted an eyebrow.

She smacked a hand into her forehead. "Stop being so incorrigible."

"Exasperating and incorrigible. I feel like I should get a gold star for forcing you to use such big words."

She shook her head, but her mouth shaped into that smile he loved so much. Then the smile dropped, and her eyes got serious. "I'm not sure why you're so patient with me. Or that I can give you what you want."

Dawson met her gaze, not allowing his to waver. "And what do I want?"

"I guess that's the question. Do you want what I think you want?"

The low chuckle rumbled in his chest. "I want you. I want your heart. I want your trust."

"What if I can't ever freely give you those things?"

"Like you said, I'm a patient man. Until you tell me to go away, I'll keep trying."

Letty looked away from him then, her gaze skittering over a dozen different things behind him somewhere before coming back to rest on his face again. "I kind of want those things, too. I just don't quite know how to get there. It's like having a broken GPS or something. I know it's there, and it should be easy to find, but I keep getting redirected to an empty field."

She kind of wanted the same things he did. Warmth filled his chest and expanded outward until he had to be glowing with it. "I'll be praying for you. For your GPS. And that you find a field filled with all the best that life has to offer."

"Could you maybe pray now?"

Dawson's smile nearly hurt, it was so big. Letty might not think she'd let him in, but asking him to pray? That was intimacy. She was letting him closer to her heart with every passing day. She might not see it as one, but as far as he was concerned, it was a victory. A huge victory. Instead of saying all of that, though, he nodded. "Absolutely."

SALLY RUSHED INTO HEAVENLY BREW, a distraught Audrey in her arms.

The high schoolers hadn't hit yet, so the line was nonexistent. Mother and daughter reached the register in record time.

Dawson was at a nearby table enjoying a late lunch when Audrey spotted him. She simultaneously reached for him and burst into tears. He was on his feet in a flash, grabbing the little girl from Sally. "What happened?"

Letty, eyes wide, came around the counter. She stood close, rubbing a hand up and down Audrey's back as Dawson held the girl. Her eyes went to Sally. "What's wrong?"

Sally, hand trembling, pushed the hair out of her eyes. "There was an accident. I don't have all the details, but Zoey's daughter Wren is in the... uh..." She glanced at her daughter. "She's in the H-O-S-P-I-T-A-L."

Audrey's cries got louder. She might not know what her mom had spelled, but she knew enough. "We need.... We need... We need..." She finally gave up trying to speak and buried her tear-and-snot-stained face against Dawson's shoulder.

He smoothed her hair and hugged her close. "It's going to be okay, sweet girl. Everything's going to be okay."

Sally pulled out her wallet. "We need every food Wren likes. Whatever she convinces her mom to order when she's here. We're going to take them to the... place. I know we won't be able to see her, but I can't sit by and just watch my kid fall apart like this."

Letty stepped away from Audrey to give Sally a hug. "Are you sure she's the only one falling apart?"

Sally took a deep shuddering breath. "She's all I have. I forget how breakable little girls are and how fragile life is. I just... I can't sit by and do nothing."

Dawson gave the girl in his arms a little jiggle. "Do you know what Wren's favorite foods are?"

Audrey sniffed. "She likes brownies and chocolate chip cookies and chocolate cake and chocolate pie and hot cocoa..."

Sally eyed her daughter. "Are you sure those aren't all of your favorites?"

Letty slipped behind the counter and started packing food into boxes and from there into two paper bags. "Here you go. Some of Wren's favorites, but also some food for Zoey, Mr. Matthews, and Connor, just in case he's there, too."

Sally took the bags in one hand while reaching for her daughter with the other. "Thank you. For the food." She glanced Dawson's way and winced. "And the shoulder to cry on."

Dawson nodded. "Tell them we're praying."

Letty stepped up next to him and leaned against his side. "And let us know if they need anything."

Dawson couldn't help but wrap an arm around Letty, pulling her in even closer. Together, they waved as Sally and Audrey slipped out the front of Heavenly Brew.

The door had no sooner closed when Letty spoke. "I'm ready to meet your mom. And..." She took a deep breath. "And the attorney guy."

The arm he had around her tightened instinctively before he loosened it and turned to face her. "Are you sure?"

She gave him a nod. "I've been meaning to say it for a few days, but I keep avoiding it. We're kind of in this happy little bubble, and I'm afraid of ruining it."

He hooked a finger under her chin and tilted her face up enough so that he could see her eyes clearly. "Life happens all the time. Bubbles always get popped, whether they're happy or sad. The foundation underneath is what really matters."

Letty held his gaze, her eyes softening. "I know. And I'm ready to start putting in some effort on that foundation."

The certainty in her gaze sent electrical impulses skittering under Dawson's skin. "Can I kiss you now?"

Color bloomed on her cheeks, but she nodded. "I'd like that."

Dawson leaned in, brushing his lips across Letty's in the lightest of kisses before returning for a second taste and then a third.

When the cowbell announced someone had stepped into the shop, Dawson pulled back enough to drop a kiss on Letty's forehead.

If they were alone, he'd tell her he loved her. He couldn't deny the emotion that had taken up residence in his chest. He loved her with his whole heart, with his whole being. But this wasn't the time or place to tell her.

Instead, he pulled out his phone and typed a text to his mom. LETTY WOULD LIKE TO MEET YOU.

"I HAVE someone I'd like you to meet." Dawson held Letty's cold hand in his own.

Letty took a step back. "I think there are some dishes..."

Philip poked his nose into the conversation. "The dishes are washed enough. Go deal with whatever it is. I've got you covered."

She looked from Philip to Dawson and then back at Philip.

The older man waved a plastic knife. "I can do some real damage with this thing if you need me to. If Dawson or the lady get out of hand, just give me the word."

Letty huffed. "Cutting the customers is bad for business, old man."

Philip's threat had done the trick, though.

As Letty wiped her hands on her jeans and squared her shoulders, Dawson looked over her head to Philip and mouthed *thank you*.

Then they were moving toward the small table set for four, and his mother wasn't the only person seated at it.

"Mom, I'd like you to meet Letty. Letty, this is my mom, Angelina Bauer."

28

"It's a pleasure to meet you again." Dawson's mom held out her hand to shake Letty's.

Letty stared for a minute, panic scratching at her from the inside. She beat it back, though, and extended her own hand. "The pleasure's mine."

Mrs. Bauer's laugh sounded like a delicate windchime caught in a summer breeze. "I couldn't help myself before. That day when I first showed up in your quaint little coffee shop. I wanted to meet the woman that had my son so..."

Dawson coughed.

The woman's eyes practically sparkled as she looked at her son. Then her attention shifted to the other man at their table, and the laughter fell away. "I brought someone to meet you."

Letty's eyes shifted to the other man at their corner table.

That man stood and held his hand out to her. "Eric Carlisle. It's a joy to meet you again."

"Again?"

He nodded. "We've met a few times, though it's been several years. I was your father's attorney."

Letty took a step back, but Dawson stood between her and

escape. Not that she felt trapped. If anything, she felt safer having him there. In his own way, he was guarding her back, protecting her.

She'd known this meeting was coming, and she'd tried to mentally prepare for it. The truth, though, was that on a normal day, she barely had the energy for small talk. And today was anything but normal. Her attention laser-focused on the attorney, she cut right to the point. "Why are you here?"

Mr. Carlisle gave her a small nod before retaking his seat. "Please sit. There are some matters relating to your father's estate that need to be settled."

Letty shook her head even as she sank into a seat.

Dawson pulled his seat close to hers and rested a hand on her knee as he spoke for her ears only. "We'll stay as long as you want. The moment you need this to be done, say the word."

Some of the tension slipped from her shoulders. Without even recognizing it, she'd started to feel trapped. Would her default always be to run when she felt cornered?

The attorney cleared his throat. "Miss Stanton..."

"Letty."

The attorney nodded and started again. "Letty, I'm the executor of your father's will, and there are some things I need to discuss with you in relation to that. Before we get to that, though, there are other things I think you ought to know, and I might be the only person with this knowledge."

Letty's hands clenched in her lap. Dawson lifted his hand from her knee, reaching over to cover her fisted ones instead. The squeeze he gave them was comforting, and she needed all the comfort she could get.

She nodded to Mr. Carlisle despite the urge to make a break for it. "Go ahead."

The older man's eyes shone as he spoke. "Some time before

your father's death, he began to suspect that your mother might be... ah... treating you poorly."

Letty blinked but said nothing. That didn't compute with her memories. Surely if her dad had understood the depth of what was going on, he would have done something. By not telling him, she'd been protecting him.

She'd also been protecting herself, though. A part of her had always feared that her dad wouldn't believe her, that he would take her mom's side just like everyone else had. So she'd taken the easy way out. She'd stayed silent and had chosen to believe he would have done something if he'd known. It would have broken her to tell him and have him not care. Yet, if Mr. Carlisle was correct, her dad had known... and it had changed nothing for her.

Letty's heart cracked, and the pain she'd carried around all these years began to seep out.

The attorney wasn't done, though. "It would have been easier if there were outright signs of abuse, but there weren't, and when he spoke to you about it, you always denied that anything was wrong."

"I don't remember him asking." Her voice was small, tentative.

"He... needed to be cautious. He asked you in subtle ways. How was your mom while he was away? Were you looking forward to your mother/daughter spa day? You never gave a glimmer that anything was wrong, but his suspicions wouldn't be quieted. So he placed some cameras in your home. Hidden cameras. He called them nanny cams."

Letty's eyes widened and her spine stiffened. "He never said." He never stopped it.

Sadness saturated the attorney's gaze. "Your dad wasn't just my client. He was my friend, too. You were his priority. He deeply regretted that he allowed himself to get so busy with work that he missed the signs of trouble. And he regretted that you didn't feel you could go to him. If the cameras had caught outright abuse, it would have been easier. So much easier."

The older man took a drink of his coffee before continuing. "The cameras didn't give us anything conclusive, though. The prenuptial agreement had, among other things, required joint custody for any children should the marriage dissolve. We needed something ironclad to make sure your dad could walk away from the marriage and maintain sole custody of you. Things are different today, but back then, custody hearings almost always favored the mom. Your dad wanted to protect you even though he blamed himself for the fact that you needed protection."

"Sole custody." Of their own volition, the words slipped from between her lips. He'd wanted sole custody. To protect her. He'd wanted to get her away from her mom. And keep her away. He'd wanted to protect her. Her dad...

She almost doubled over with the pain of it.

Her dad had wanted to protect her when she'd been too afraid to tell him she needed protecting.

The attorney's gaze was sympathetic as he gave her a minute.

Those seeping emotions were starting to turn into a torrent, but she managed a nod.

Mr. Carlisle continued. "Because the cameras didn't give us what we'd hoped, we had to start the process of untangling the estates. Your dad wanted to give you a space where you would be physically safe, but he also wanted to provide for you and make sure that you were financially secure. He didn't want you to ever be at your mother's mercy again. We spent months working on getting everything in order so that he could walk away from his marriage and take you with him. I was set to file the divorce papers on Friday."

Letty's gaze flew from her lap to the attorney's eyes. "Friday?"

He nodded. "Two days after your seventeenth birthday."

"I never knew."

"He'd planned to talk to you about it on your birthday."

"My birthday?" Letty's voice cracked. Her seventeenth birthday was forever burned into her mind and soul. After all, it was the day she'd killed her father.

The attorney, apparently unaware that her entire world was imploding, carried on. "He bought you that car against your mom's wishes so you would always have a means of escape, even if that meant you wanted to escape from him once everything came out. He was supposed to take you to see the condo he'd purchased for the two of you. It was near your school."

"Condo?" Letty again echoed the attorney.

Mr. Carlisle nodded.

Letty shook her head. "He said where we were going was a surprise."

The shadows under the man's eyes seemed to deepen as he sat there. "He wanted to file for divorce sooner, but I advised against it. I wanted him to give his legal team time to make sure he could extricate himself from your mother as easily as possible. He held off on filing under my advice and against his better judgment. If I had just done what he'd wanted, if he'd filed when he wanted, your dad would still be here with us. It's my fault that he's gone, and that is a burden of guilt I will carry every day for the rest of my life."

Letty shook her head. "I was driving. It's my fault. Mom said..."

The attorney's eyebrow lifted. "She said...?"

"She said I was at fault. The police were opening an investigation. I might be indicted for murder. Or manslaughter. Or something. I don't remember exactly, but she kept telling me that I'd killed my father. I was the reason he was dead." Grief blanketed Letty like a dense fog over a crystalline lake.

Mr. Carlisle shook his head sharply, his now-fisted hands resting on the table. "The car's computer showed that you braked. You hit the brakes, but the command to brake was never sent to the car's operating system. You flew through that intersection, but it wasn't your fault."

This had Dawson sitting up straighter beside her. "How could that happen?"

The attorney kept his eyes on Letty as he answered the question. "We don't know if the car malfunctioned or if the operating system was hacked. If I'm being honest, I had hoped to find evidence incriminating your mom. We couldn't find anything conclusive, though. I don't know why the car didn't brake, but I know with absolute certainty that your dad's death never rested on your shoulders."

Letty swiped at a wayward tear. All that pain seeping out of her heart was now seeping out of her eyes, too.

The attorney waited until Letty raised her eyes and met his gaze. "Your dad loved you so very much, and he never would have wanted for you to blame yourself."

Letty straightened her shoulders, clinging to the knowledge that her dad had fought for her even though she hadn't known it at the time. "He didn't have to take your advice. It's not your fault, either."

Mr. Carlisle sat back and offered a half-smile. "We can agree to disagree."

"How long? From when he first noticed until..." Her words died off, her will to ask them wavering.

"It took him a little while from when he first suspected something to deciding that his suspicions weren't crazy. From when he first came to me with it — he wanted to know if he could legally put cameras in his own home — until the day I was supposed to file the divorce papers? Four months."

"He was home more toward the end. I didn't know why, but I loved having him there."

"Your dad was CEO of the company your maternal grandfather founded. He was likely to lose his position in the divorce. As soon as he started to have suspicions, he began training his replacement. He knew what was coming, and it was worth it to him. You were worth it."

Shell-shocked didn't even begin to describe Letty's state of mind.

The noise in the coffee shop ebbed and flowed. The cowbell clanged each time the door opened. Dishes banged and the espresso machine hissed and steamed. Nothing around them had changed, not really. Yet Letty sat there. Her whole world — or what she thought she knew of it — had crumbled. And she didn't know how to put it back together.

Fine tremors shook her body as Dawson leaned close. "Do you want to go? We can finish this later."

Letty didn't have to look at him. She just nodded. "Please."

Before she could say a word to Mrs. Bauer or Mr. Carlisle, Dawson had hustled the two of them out the front door of Heavenly Brew and turned them in the direction of his car.

Was she running away from a problem again? Yes.

But not permanently. She needed to catch her breath and process what she'd learned before she could pack anything more on top of it.

And this time, she wasn't alone. She might have been running away, but she was doing it with Dawson at her side.

She wouldn't have it any other way.

29

Dawson kept silent vigil over Letty as he drove them through town before making a break for the flat winter-wrapped landscape beyond the city limits.

Letty's knuckles were a stark white against the dark denim of her jeans, but at least the trembling had eased off to nothing more than an occasional shudder.

After nearly an hour, the tension visibly eased from Letty's muscles and she found her voice. "Mr. Carlisle said there's more, but what more could there be?"

Dawson cleared his throat. How much more could she take? "I would assume you have an inheritance. He first introduced himself as the executor of your dad's will. He may have wanted to get the personal stuff done first."

"An inheritance?" Her voice was hollow, but it could have been worse.

Dawson cast a glance her way. She was staring back, listening. "I don't know the details, but based on what he said today, I'd imagine that during those four months when your dad tried to get things squared away, he would have done something to tie up your inheritance so your mom couldn't get her hands on it.

But that's just a guess. Otherwise... I mean... did your mom never try to find you? If she could prove she'd tried to find you and couldn't, she could have had you declared legally dead, right? I couldn't find any record of that, though. I looked. After I figured out who you were. I wanted to understand what had happened..."

Letty shifted in the passenger seat, turning her body to face his. "I don't really know... I spent the first few years living in fear every day that she would show up, but after a while I stopped worrying about it. Around year six, I kind of figured she was never coming, and I was glad. Relieved."

They arrived at a deserted T-intersection, and Dawson turned the car around. "You changed your name, but your Social Security number is probably the same, too. If she'd really wanted to find you, she could have."

"Philip hired an investigator early on to figure out my iden-tity and what I'd run from. He didn't go into details about what he found, but in the end, he had the investigator do something — something designed to lead someone on a wild goose chase if they searched for me."

Dawson kept his eyes on the road. "That makes sense, and something like that might have held up under a cursory search, but the moment you filed taxes, if someone really looked, they could have found you."

"That would involve hacking the IRS, right? Nobody's that dumb." She wished she felt as confident on the matter as she sounded.

"Or bribing an IRS official. Which I'm not condoning. But if your mom had hired someone to find you, and if they were any good at their job, they'd have found you. So why didn't she? Did she never look? Or did she learn your whereabouts and ignore it until my mom and I shook some trees? None of it makes sense."

Letty bit her bottom lip. "Ugh. I like simple. Why does all of this have to be so convoluted?"

Dawson threw a quick glance her way. He could stare at her all day if he let himself, but the road needed his attention, too. "I'm not sure, but I do know God's in control and that He is good."

"So good He let my father die?"

"Would you wish your father back?"

Would she? Would she wish him back to this earth? To the broken and fallen world in which she lived? Would she wish him back to dealing with her mom? To all the hurt and heartache that had to come with realizing the woman you married isn't a very good person after all?

"If I could wish him back for one more hug, I would. But the rest? I don't know if he was saved. We went to church, but for my mom, it was all about appearances. I don't know if it ever meant more to Dad. The thought of him dying an unbeliever is... hard. It's hard."

This was something he could actually help with. This was not exactly a smiling conversation, but he threw one Letty's way regardless. "What if I could help allay those fears?"

She wrapped her arms around her middle. "What do you mean?"

Dawson tapped a button on his steering wheel, and when the car beeped, he said, "Call Dad."

The phone's ringing came through the car's sound system, and after the third ring, a rich voice answered. "Hey, kiddo. Good to hear from you. Are you keeping your mom out of trouble?"

Dawson rolled his eyes. "Hey, Dad. You're on speaker. And, um, if you can't do that, what makes you think I can?"

His dad's chuckle reminded him of home. "Okay, then. What can I help you with?"

Dawson reached over and brushed a finger down Letty's cheek. "I have Letty Stanton with me. We were just talking about her dad — Mr. Stanley — and whether or not he was a believer. Could you tell her what you told me?"

"Oh... yeah. Sure." Dad's rich voice had hints of the Bay Area bleeding through it despite his years in the Midwest.

Silence settled in the car until Dawson prompted his dad. "Go ahead."

"Yeah, yeah. Sorry. This would be easier in person. It's nice to meet you, Letty. Or meet you again, I guess. I know it's been a long time, but I'm sorry for your loss."

"Thank you. It's nice to... um... meet you, too."

Dawson's dad chuckled. "Dawson called the other day to ask if I remember anything about your parents. I never knew your mom that well, but your dad and I attended a men's Bible study together. We met Thursday mornings at the ridiculous hour of five o'clock. Your dad traveled a lot for work, so he couldn't make it every week, but when he was in town, he always came. If you ever want to know some of the details of things we talked about, I can share them with you. The main thing, I guess, is that your dad was a man of tremendous faith. He started attending the study about a year before he died. He'd only recently come to Christ, and he didn't know how to live out his faith in his family or with his job. I saw him grow in many ways during that year. Christ became his bedrock, though, and he was shifting everything in his life so that it was built on that bedrock. It was bumpy and not always pretty, and he got pushback in his marriage and at work, but his faith was so solid it was practically a living, breathing thing."

Dawson pulled off to the side of the road. "Thanks, Dad. I'll give you a call later."

"Sure, kiddo. Love you."

"Love you, too."

And the call was over.

Beside him, Letty sank further into the seat as the sharp edges of her tension softened.

Letty sat there in the silence, and Dawson didn't rush in to fill it. Knowing her dad had been a believer had to be good news, but it was still a lot to absorb.

"He never told me. It shouldn't hurt that he kept it from me, but..."

Dawson reached over and clasped one of her hands in his. "Don't take it personally. He had a lot to deal with, and I'm sure he planned to tell you. He wouldn't have kept that from you. He might have even felt that he needed to get you away from your mother first. Don't judge him too harshly."

"No, I wouldn't."

"Wouldn't...?"

Letty took a deep breath and released it slowly. When she looked up at Dawson, her eyes were clearer than he'd ever seen. They practically shone with an inner light.

"Is this what peace feels like?" She tilted her head to the side and studied him. "I'm not sure I've ever felt like this before. So..."

"Light?"

She smiled. "Yeah. Light."

It shouldn't have been possible for her to be any more magnetic than she already was, but that smile... Her smile was full of joy, full of hope. It held the promise of tomorrow. "I'm happy you found some of the answers you needed."

Letty rested her free hand on top of his. "I wish things had been different. I wish I could have done things differently. I wish my dad and I had talked more. But, no. Knowing where he is, I would never wish him back to this world or this life. Even if it hurts to say that."

That question had been a while ago, but it did his heart good to hear her so confidently answer it now. "You're one of the bravest people I've ever met, you know that?"

"Ha. I'm just the girl who runs away."

He chuckled as he put the car back into gear. "When are you going to learn?"

30

Maybe Dawson was right. She hadn't just run away. She'd run *to* something.

She might have run away from her mother and her past and the pain of it all, but she'd run to a place where she could breathe and feel and experience life... and find the Christ whose peace now reigned in her heart.

Dawson pulled the car into the driveway of his rental.

Letty unbuckled her seatbelt. "I guess it would have been weird for them to stay at Heavenly Brew."

He offered her a shrug. "We can go in there and finish the conversation with Mr. Carlisle if you want. Or I can take you somewhere else."

Letty stepped out of the car and clasped his hand as soon as he got close enough. "You're so warm. My hands are always cold."

He couldn't help the smile. "Are you changing the subject?"

Her lips twitched before she grew somber. "I don't actually care about any inheritance."

Dawson stared at his still-closed garage door before glancing down at her with gentleness in his eyes. "Your father loved you and cared for you and made some sort of provision for you in his will. If you go in there and face whatever Carlisle has to say, you're accepting whatever your dad did for you, knowing that he did it out of love. If you walk away, I guess in a way, you're kind of robbing him of the right to take care of his daughter. I'm not saying he took care of you perfectly or that he couldn't or shouldn't have done things differently, but this — his will — is his very last means of caring for you."

"Ouch. Guilt much?"

His brows drew together. "I wasn't going for guilt."

"I know." She took two steps toward his front door before stopping again. "Do you think he could just send me a letter?"

"Maybe. Probably. But he made the effort to fly out here to see you personally. This is important to him, maybe even more important than it is to you."

Tremors shook Letty's hands. "I'm not as brave as you seem to think."

Dawson leaned over into Letty's space, whispering his words against the shell of her ear. "Your bravery is beautiful, but just in case you forget for a minute just how brave you are, I'll be here to remind you."

She turned her head enough to drop a kiss on the corner of his mouth. "Let's do this."

Dawson palmed his keys as they approached the front door. "I've got you."

She didn't utter a word, but she did walk tall as they entered the house and made their way toward the voices in the kitchen.

Mrs. Bauer and Mr. Carlisle were sitting at the dining room table, and Philip stood there, arms crossed, as he glared at them.

As soon as Philip saw Letty, his face relaxed. "Don't worry about the shop. Mrs. B will keep it flying right."

Letty shrugged. "She doesn't even know how to use the espresso machine."

"But she knows who does." Philip winked. He wasn't usually a winker. He didn't often let out the inner teddy bear that he hid somewhere under his crusty barnacle-covered exterior.

Dawson's mom rose to her feet. "Letty, dear, can I get you some coffee? Or tea? Or... oh." A blush stained her cheeks. "I guess if you make that stuff for a living, anything I'd make probably wouldn't compare."

Letty pulled out a chair from the kitchen table and sat. "I don't need anything right now, thank you. But for the record, I'm not fussy, either."

Mrs. Bauer nodded, her eyes on Letty. "Do you want us to leave you alone for this?"

Did she? If she and Dawson were going to be a thing, then his family would sort of become her family eventually. And Philip was already family. So... "I don't imagine it matters."

Dawson's mom glanced at him, eyebrows lifted. She didn't strike Letty as someone who was normally unsure of herself. When Dawson nodded to her, though, she resumed her seat at the table. "If you change your mind, dear, and want us to go, you only need to say the word."

Philip sat on Letty's other side, all signs of the teddy bear gone as his grim stare took in the attorney's every move.

For his part, Mr. Carlisle seemed relatively unaffected. He reached for the old-school briefcase that sat by his feet and lifted it to the table before opening it. He withdrew a dappled brown file folder from the interior, then relatched the briefcase and returned it to the floor. He cleared his throat before opening the folder and looking at Letty. "As soon as your father realized what was going on and began the process of separating his assets from your mother's, he rewrote his will, naming you his sole beneficiary. However, everything went into a trust to be released to you on your thirtieth birthday. The funds could also be released to you sooner under certain circumstances."

Letty nodded but didn't ask what those circumstances might be.

The attorney continued. "If you passed away before you reached your majority, the entire estate would go to charity. Your father designated five charities."

Letty tilted her head. "My mother wouldn't get it?"

Carlisle shook his head. "Which is why she never made any move to have you declared dead."

One question answered, at least.

"Because you were a minor when your father passed, your mother was your legal guardian. I was named executor of his will, but she was your guardian. She hired a team of attorneys to fight the will, saying that she should have access to funds so that she could care for you until you came into the funds at age thirty. The attorneys also argued early on that funds were needed to search for you. Your mother put on quite the theatrical performance in the courtroom. She portrayed herself as a grieving widow who was heartbroken over her daughter's disappearance."

"And the judge fell for it?"

The older man nodded. "When I tried to submit the video recordings from your home, her attorneys moved to suppress the evidence. Ultimately, the judge ruled in their favor."

"So my mom's been draining this trust fund?"

Mr. Carlisle chuckled. "Your mother has absolutely no idea how much your father was worth. She was the one who came from money, and it never occurred to her that he might have accumulated his own wealth along the way. She has barely scratched the surface of your trust. While I couldn't completely block her from access, I could take certain steps."

"Such as?"

"For starters, she has never seen a balance sheet on the trust fund. She gets a monthly allowance deposited directly into her account, and that's it. In addition to her monthly allowance, though, she had unlimited access to the necessary funds to search for you. The PI she'd been using passed away about three years ago, and when she tried to hire a new one, she happened to reach out to a PI that I sometimes use. Mrs. Stanley asked the woman to falsify receipts with the promise that she would split the proceeds with her. The PI brought the tale to me, and I went to the judge. Her testimony convinced the judge to demand your mother turn over all investigative reports from the previous PI. When she couldn't — because there were no reports — and when two more investigators came forward to say she'd approached them, too, the judge pulled the funding from her search for you."

Dawson's foot tapped out a fast beat on the floor. "If she came from money, why did Letty's mom need to go after the trust fund?"

Mr. Carlisle's lips tipped up. "In the weeks following the car accident, it came to light that Letty's grandfather had been embezzling from his own company."

Philip offered a dark chuckle.

"What happened?" Letty barely remembered her maternal grandparents. They'd never been particularly warm.

The attorney watched Letty as he answered. "Your grandparents' assets were frozen, and by the time the case made its way through the criminal and civil courts, they had nothing left. Any money that your mom might have one day inherited was gone. Your trust fund became her only source of income."

Philip grunted. "If you ask me, the woman should have gone and gotten herself a job."

Nobody argued.

Letty took a deep breath and asked the question burning in her heart. "Why didn't you search for me?"

The color drained from the old man's already-pale cheeks.

"Your guy here—" He tipped his head toward Philip. "He did a pretty good job of covering your tracks. Then I had a battle with colon cancer. Then they found a tumor in my wife's brain. The last decade hasn't been very calm in my world. As soon as we got things cleared up three years ago, I put the PI who testified on the job. She found you last year right as my wife had a relapse. I told myself you were safe and that you'd be okay until I could give you the attention you deserved."

Letty could have said so many things. Some of them weren't particularly nice. In the end, though... "It's all in God's timing, I guess. Who knows? If you'd come to me sooner, I might not have met Dawson."

Dawson leaned close. "You have a kind heart."

She ignored him and spoke again to the attorney. "Is your wife okay?"

Mr. Carlisle's eyes instantly flooded with tears. He swiped at them with shaking hands. "We buried her the month before last."

The man's grief landed a blow to Letty's gut. Despite the time that had passed, her grief for her father still felt fresh, and the attorney's pain only brought hers into sharper focus.

One of these days she would need to let herself properly grieve. The time might finally be right to start letting go.

31

W ell, then.

Dawson couldn't exactly harbor any anger toward the man who could have set Letty free from her self-imposed exile.

Not only had the man's wife — a wife he clearly still loved — just died, but Letty had been right. If Mr. Carlisle had acted sooner, Letty might not have been in Gilead when he'd accepted the job at the college. He would rest in the peace of knowing God had allowed things to happen how and when they had happened.

And he would know happiness. Because having Letty in his life was worth being forced to forgive and let something go when he might have rather held onto a little bit of a grudge.

"I'm so sorry for your loss." Letty's words pulled him out of his head where he'd apparently gotten stuck.

"No. No. I'm the one who's sorry." Mr. Carlisle's words of apology settled into the air between them like a balloon in the ocean, barely staying afloat as more waves bore down on it.

Letty shook her head, cutting the attorney off. "I've learned a few things in the years I've been in Gilead. I've learned that God is sovereign. I've learned that His love for His people knows no bounds and that He knows what is best and right and good even when it doesn't make a lot of sense to us. I needed to be here."

The attorney offered a sad smile. "I appreciate your perspective, but I'm not sure *need* is the right word for it."

"I'm sure. If I hadn't ended up in Gilead, I wouldn't have Philip. I wouldn't have Heavenly Brew. I wouldn't have the friends and family I've found in this little corner of the world, and those people are the ones who helped me to recover from my father's death and to forgive myself for the part I played in it. If I hadn't ended up in Gilead, I... I wouldn't be who I am today, and while I still have a lot to work on, I'm freer and happier than I've ever been."

Dawson reached under the table and rested a hand on her knee. She reached down and laced her fingers through his, and a thrill of pure electric joy shot through him.

Letty continued speaking to the attorney, her voice steadier than ever. "Despite the sadness and hardship I've faced along the way, God has blessed me. He's carried me through the hard times, and He has blessed me immeasurably. So don't apologize anymore and don't blame yourself. For all we know, if you'd come for me sooner, things would have ended up worse instead of better."

Mr. Carlisle offered a watery smile. "You're wise beyond your years. You get that from your dad."

Philip leaned his elbows on the table with a bit of a thunk. "So just how much are we talking about in this trust fund?"

Letty snorted and shoved the older man's shoulder with her free hand.

The attorney dabbed at his eyes one last time before flipping through some of the papers in the folder. He came to a balance sheet and passed it over to Letty. "That's current as of yesterday."

Her eyes popped wider than he'd ever seen. On any person. Ever.

Philip made a choking sound.

As for Dawson, he laughed. What else was he supposed to do? His mind was officially blown.

After a while, Letty found her voice. "My dad was worth... that much?"

Mr. Carlisle gave her the first real smile any of them had seen from him. "As the executor, I had the freedom to invest a portion of the funds each year. I could never invest more than twenty percent in a given year, and no more than fifty percent of that could be in any sort of unguaranteed investment at a time."

"So you played the stock market with her trust fund?" Dawson looked at the attorney in a new light. Maybe the guy had missed his calling when he became an attorney.

Mr. Carlisle chuckled. "Not exactly, but close enough. Even with your mother's allowance, you're up almost thirty percent since the trust fund was established."

Philip nudged her with his elbow. "You can afford to buy out Heavenly Brew now."

Letty shrugged but wouldn't meet Philip's gaze. "I kind of like having a partner."

The older man's voice was gruff as always. "Are you going to make it worth my while?"

Letty laughed, and the tension visibly eased from her shoulders. "You're not fooling anyone, Philip. We all know how much you've enjoyed being back in the shop on the regular."

"You're out of your ever-loving mind."

Dawson leaned forward and speared Philip with a look, even though his words were for Letty. "He started a rumor that Mrs. Alleghany is moving to Alaska. Mr. Abrams danced a little jig with his cane when he heard."

Letty giggled. An actual girly giggle. And it. Was. Breathtaking.

Nothing would ever compare to life in Gilead, Kansas. To life with Letty.

Philip tapped his fingers on the table. "So what are these conditions? She's not thirty yet, after all. That may be a lot of money, but it won't do her any good locked up in a trust fund."

The attorney thumbed through the papers in the folder before pulling one out and sliding it across to her. "I need to do a blood test to confirm your identity via DNA. Once that's taken care of, you'll receive a monthly allowance of $15,000. If you have a large purchase you need to make prior to your thirtieth birthday, you just need to provide documentation to me, and I will make the decision whether or not to approve it. If you want access to the full amount before you turn thirty..."

"No." Letty cut him off. "Nope. Not happening. I can't even wrap my mind around the numbers you're saying right now. There's no way I'll need more sooner."

Mr. Carlisle nodded. "Okay. If you change your mind, though, the conditions are listed there on that paper."

Dawson's eyes dropped of their own volition, and he read the page with Letty and Philip.

CONDITIONS TO BE MET *for early release of trust fund:*

1. *Must be humble in character and deed.*
2. *Must demonstrate kindness even when she thinks no one is watching.*
3. *Must show herself to be a good judge of character or be able to rely on people who are. (Money makes people want to take advantage of you. She needs to have discernment*

> *about these things or have people in her life who can help*
> *protect her.)*
>
> 4. *Must be actively earning her own income apart from her*
>   *trust fund allowance.*

"This is…" Her words trailed off.

Dawson was pretty sure he knew what she'd been about to say. "This isn't remotely standard."

Philip tapped the paper with a blunt finger. "This here is a father's wish about the kind of woman his daughter would grow up to be."

Tears spilled over and chased each other down Letty's cheeks. She swiped at them as her chin trembled. "My heart is so full right now."

Dawson's mom had been mostly silent through the entire exchange, but she'd taken in every word. He met his mom's gaze even though his words weren't directed at her. "It's good to be surrounded by so much love, isn't it?"

32

Letty swiped more tears away. "Yes."

She was surrounded by more love than she'd ever realized.

Yet her heart broke anew.

She would need to grieve again for her father, but it would be different. This time around, she would be grieving for a man who hadn't been blind to what was going on and who had been taking steps to protect her. This time, her grief would be unstained by guilt, unstained by shame, unstained by self-blame. This time, her grief would be painted with the brush of hope, eternal hope. She would see her father again someday.

This was not the end. She would see him again.

How had she survived the grief the first time when she'd had no idea? When eternal hope hadn't even been in her vocabulary?

Ah. The truth was, she hadn't survived. She'd carried that brokenness inside of her for years. She'd powered through, and she'd found forgiveness in Christ, but she'd never truly healed. Hence not letting anyone close enough to cause her pain.

Sally had been right about her not setting down roots, about not letting people close to her heart.

God was so, so good. He'd brought her farther than she'd ever dreamed and given her more hope than she knew how to handle. He'd given her father back to her, too.

And He'd made sure that, this time, she wouldn't be grieving alone.

"So, what do you think of life now that you have some free nights?" Letty glanced sideways at Dawson. A lesser man would have picked a woman with a simpler history. He continued to spend time with her, though. That had to count for something.

He reached for her hand and threaded his fingers through hers. "I'm glad rehearsals are over. It gives me time for other worthy causes."

They were walking from Heavenly Brew — where Philip had given them stink-eye — to a nearby diner. Letty didn't often get an evening off. Until Dawson, she'd never really wanted one. "Such as?"

He gave her hand a squeeze before opening the diner's door for her. "If you have to ask, I'm doing something wrong."

She didn't bother putting up much resistance when the smile pulled at her lips. If the look on Dawson's face was anything to go by, he appreciated her smile.

They settled into a booth and pulled menus from the holder, companionable silence surrounding them.

"Well, I never..." Mrs. Alleghany's voice intruded even though she wasn't speaking to them.

"All I'm saying is, mind your own business. You don't need to share your opinion on everything and everybody." The man's voice was loud enough to be heard throughout the dining area.

"Is that...?" Dawson's eyebrows were raised.

"Frank. From Sunday school." Letty answered the unfinished question.

"I wonder what... Nope. Never mind. Not our business." Dawson put his nose back in his menu, and Letty followed suit, stifling a giggle.

One of these days, someone was going to put Mrs. Alleghany in her place, and it would be in a way the woman couldn't ignore.

"What'll it be?" The waitress stood there, order pad in hand and smile firmly in place despite Mrs. Alleghany's ongoing mutterings at the cash register.

After they ordered and the waitress retreated, Dawson reached across the table and recaptured her hand. "Who knew we'd get dinner and a show?"

Letty winced as Mrs. Alleghany walked past them, eyes lingering on their clasped hands, on her way to the exit. "I think we may have just become the show."

"Is that a problem?"

She looked at the man across from her. His eyes held questions. Uncertainty. She hadn't exactly been a steady rock since he'd come to town, and maybe she'd left him guessing more than she'd meant to.

Letty pulled her hand from Dawson's, placed both of hers on the table between them, and leaned forward. "Come here."

He leaned in, his posture saying he expected to hear a whispered comment. Before he could turn his head to offer his ear, though, she pushed forward and kissed him. It was a quick peck. Over in a flash. But it had been on the lips. In public. In Gilead.

He eased back, his eyes searching hers. "That was... unexpected. Nice. Don't get me wrong. It was very, very, very nice. Just... unexpected."

"You asked if it was a problem that Mrs. Alleghany saw us holding hands."

Those beautiful cinnamon eyes lit up. "I guess this means it's not a problem?"

"Now you're getting it."

Frank stopped by their table, a grin on his face. "Thanks for taking the heat off me. No one's going to remember me snapping at a little old lady. You'll be all anyone can talk about."

The satisfaction on Dawson's face made Letty's toes curl. "Any time, man. Any time."

MR. ABRAMS EYED LETTY's left hand. "No ring yet, huh?"

Mr. Williams, next in line, spoke up. "From what I hear, y'all were practically making babies in the middle of the diner. You should lock him down, Letty, before someone scares him away."

"Scares him away!? Hush up, you old fool. Have you even seen the way he looks at our girl?" Mr. Abrams pounded his cane for good measure.

Cici, ever the faithful and silent hard worker, popped up next to Letty at the register. "He's been in here every day for weeks. He just sits there mooning over Letty. He's not going anywhere."

The front door opened with the jangle of the cowbell, and Sally stepped in. "So, what's this I hear about a public make-out session?"

Letty threw her hands up in the air. "People! My love life is not on the menu!"

Mr. Abrams tapped his cane and chuckled. "At least you're finally admitting that you have a love life. Progress, my girl."

PHILIP TAPPED some buttons on the newly mounted keypad. "You've got the app installed, right?"

Letty pulled it up on her phone. "Yep. I can see everything."

He grunted. "Stay on top of it. Don't forget to turn the alarm on when you close at night."

She'd insisted that she was ready to return to her apartment above Heavenly Brew, and Philip had insisted on installing a security system and making sure all the doors and windows worked — and locked — properly.

"Got it, old man. Lock it up tight. Don't let in any strangers. Don't burn the place down."

He laughed. Outright, out loud, laughed. And Philip wasn't the laughing type. "You remember that?"

He'd given her those instructions when she'd first moved into the apartment. Every single evening as he left. *Lock it up tight. Don't let in any strangers. Don't burn the place down.*

Back then, everyone had been a stranger to her, so his mandate had been pretty much universal. Let no one in. Even when she'd insisted on buying her own lock for the apartment door because she didn't yet trust Philip, he'd looked out for her.

He started chuckling again. "Remember the first time I showed you how to use the espresso machine?"

How could she forget? When the steam had hissed, she'd hit the floor and covered her head. "I was a little skittish back then."

His laughter was gone, but a smile still shaped his mouth. "You were sunshine on a cloudy day."

What was a girl supposed to say to that?

Philip pointed at the keypad again. "Keep it armed whenever you're here alone. We don't know if that woman –" *her mother* "– is going to show up. Be smart."

Letty patted him on the shoulder. "Got it, old man. You don't need to worry about me. Don't you and the guys have your poker game tonight?"

He scowled. "Charlie took me to the cleaners last time. I need to get my money back."

"You all play with pennies. You couldn't even pay for a load at the laundromat with that. What kind of cleaners are you talking about?"

Philip threw a crumbled-up paper towel at her. "Such a smart mouth."

She stuck her tongue out at him before he started packing up his tools. The new security system hadn't needed much in the way of tools, but he'd come fully prepared regardless. Because he cared.

33

D awson stood in the church's foyer, marking time while Letty had stepped away to use the restroom.

Someone bumped into him from behind. A woman said, "Oh, I'm so sorry, dear," at the same time that a man's voice rumbled, "You'd best not make our girl cry."

Dawson had always felt generally welcome in Gilead. Ever since that day Letty had kissed him in the diner, though, he'd received more smiles, pats on the back, and random muttered threats than he would have thought possible.

Maybe the threats should have bothered him more. Some of them were more creative than others, but they all came down to one central theme. *Don't you dare hurt Letty.*

He had a sneaking suspicion that Philip was behind the threats. He had some sort of underground network of men with grumbly voices who were willing to do his bidding. It had to be Philip's doing.

Although Mr. Watersby wasn't completely above suspicion, either.

Oh, well. What was a guy to do when confronted with a town

that loved someone nearly as much as he did? Embrace it. That was the only real choice.

Letty approached, her eyes scanning his face. "Everything okay? You're doing that crazy eye thing again."

"Eh. Gilead brings out the crazy in me, I guess."

She gave him a dose of side-eye as they approached the church's exit. "You know I have enough crazy in my life already, right? You could try to be a sane influence, and I wouldn't complain."

He snorted. "Sure. Sane. That'll help me fit right in here in Gilead. I'll get right on that."

Once they stepped into the sunlight, Letty looped her hand around his arm and stepped in close to his side. "A little crazy's okay. Just don't overdo it."

Dawson would have done anything Letty asked, no doubt about it. With her at his side, he could take on the whole world if needed. What was the saying? Ten feet tall and bulletproof. Not that he planned to put that to the test any time soon, but Letty...

Her phone's ring interrupted his thoughts.

"Oh, hold on. I need to get this." She took a step away before answering.

Dawson wasn't really listening to her conversation, but the way she kept glancing at him put him on alert.

"Of course, Mrs.... I mean, of course, Lyla. Will do."

There wasn't anything necessarily weird about what she had said. Those beautiful aquamarine eyes, though, hid something.

When Letty took his hand again, he tugged her close and leaned down to whisper into her ear. "For a woman who has spent years of her life keeping secrets, you're really bad at it."

She chuckled. "You're not lying."

"Going to tell me what you've got going on?"

She squeezed his hand. "Yes. But not yet."

"Should I be worried?"

She hummed low. "I don't think so."

That didn't exactly put his heart at ease. "I'm beginning to think I don't like surprises."

"I think you'll like this one. I'm pretty sure you will. I mean..."

Dawson could have kicked himself as Letty's smile slipped away. "If you say I'm going to like it, I'm sure I'll love it."

DAWSON SMILED at the face on the screen. "Hey, Dad. Thanks for taking time. Sorry I couldn't be there in person."

"Give me a break. A chance to visit with my son? I'll take it any day of the week, even if it's via teleconference."

Dawson took a deep breath.

Dad's eyebrows lifted. "What's on your mind?"

"Remember when I proposed to Jayla? You thought I was rushing things."

"I should have kept my opinion to myself. If I'd known you two would have such a short time together, I..."

"No. You were right. I did rush it. As soon as I proposed, we started having trouble. We would have worked it out. We would have been okay. I believe that. But I let my emotions control everything, and I rushed ahead. I was so sure that I knew more than everyone else."

"Everyone?"

"You weren't the only person who told me I was moving too fast."

Dad gave a single nod. "Ah. Well, still. I wish I'd been more supportive. But tell me, why are we talking about this now?"

"I...I'm in love. So in love. Crazy in love. Ridiculously in..."

Dad chuckled. "I think I get the point. That still doesn't tell me why we're talking about Jayla when she's clearly not the woman evoking such strong emotions."

Dawson ran a hand through his hair. "I want to jump in with both feet. Full steam ahead. It feels right. It feels... different. This time feels different, but I'm not sure I can trust myself not to make the same mistake a second time."

His father leaned in close to the camera and stared straight at him. "Son, you're not the same man. Even before you met Letty, I could have told you that. You are not the same. You're more mature as a man, but more importantly, you've grown in your faith."

Dawson blinked. "I've made more mistakes than I care to admit."

"You're no longer that young man who was determined to prove to the whole world that *his* way was better than everyone else's, including God's. If you tell me that you've prayed about this and believe God is telling you Letty is the woman for you, then I have no doubt you are correct. I trust you to listen to God on this. Because that's the kind of man you've grown into."

The power of his father's words pushed Dawson back in his chair. "I don't want to mess this up, and I don't want to hurt her."

"You're going to hurt her. You're an imperfect flawed man, and she's an imperfect flawed woman. Hurt is bound to happen. It doesn't have to be the norm, though. And if I know you, it won't be the norm."

"You have a lot of faith in me."

Dad chuckled. "I also have first-hand accounts from your mom. Trust me when I tell you she's been praying for you and Letty from the very first time you texted and asked her if we knew anyone by that name."

"All this time?"

"That woman knows the men in her life better than we'd like to think."

"I guess so."

Dad lifted a single eyebrow. "So, does this mean there's an engagement in your near future?"

"No. Not yet. Definitely... I don't know. Maybe? I... have no idea. I just needed to know..."

"You have my blessing. Your mother's, too. For whatever decision you make. Yes, no. Fast, slow. Regardless, we're Team Dawson all the way."

Dawson choked. "At least you didn't put a hashtag on it."

As he was speaking, the chat box popped up with a message from Dad.

#TeamDawson

Dawson shook his head. "I feel like I've stepped into some science fiction show now. Like aliens have snatched my dad's body or something."

Dad laughed that big, loud, unrestrained laugh that Dawson had grown up hearing and loving. "Talk to you later, son. I love you."

"Love you too."

His dad's face faded from the screen, and Dawson sat back in his seat. He wasn't thinking of marriage. Not really. And yet... He couldn't think of Letty without thinking of forever. That wasn't much different, was it?

Guide my steps, God. Keep me in Your will.

Something inside him quietly snapped into place, and confidence slipped into the cracks so recently filled with insecurity.

Dawson might not know all of God's will for him, but he knew one thing with certainty. His love for Letty wasn't an accident. God had brought him to Gilead. God had put Letty in his path. Loving Letty wasn't a mistake; it was part of God's plan for his life — a part of God's plan with which he had no trouble getting on board.

Serving God and loving Letty. Was there a better way to spend his life? He couldn't think of one.

34

"Two cotton candies and a pineapple coconut shaved ice!" Marco yelled out the order.

Letty, taking her turn on the shaved ice machine, got to work. She scraped the bits of ice into the cup before pouring the flavored syrup over it.

"Thanks!" Marco practically shouted to be heard above the din as she handed him her part of the order.

Janie was right behind her with the cotton candies.

Good Friday had finally arrived. It was the last showing of the Easter production, and the people had come out in droves. Some people believed the Good Friday showing was better somehow. Maybe they were right. Others, though, had simply procrastinated since opening night on Ash Wednesday. Regardless, the show had sold out days before, and the line to the concession stand wound without end through the lobby.

Two girls from the college placed their order with Marco before picking back up with their conversation. Eavesdropping on customers wasn't Letty's go-to, but as soon as the girls mentioned Becky, she stopped her retreat.

"Can you believe Becky's dating Logan Miles?"

The other girl snorted. "According to Mrs. Alleghany, she goes by Bek. But nobody can find the news article she's talking about."

"Yeah, but it was an Australian newspaper, and you know Logan Miles could bury it if he wanted to."

"What is it about famous people always being called by first and last name? Why is that even a thing?"

"He's Logan Miles. Duh. Besides, Blogan is a terrible couple's name."

"Logek isn't any better."

Both girls burst into laughter.

Marco was about to hand the girls their drinks when Letty took them out of his hands and gave him a light hip-check to get him out of the way. She should hold her tongue. She should absolutely not say anything. And yet... "Listen, girls. You shouldn't listen to whatever Mrs. Alleghany has to say. It may seem harmless to you now, but as soon as she turns her gossip against you, you'll know just how destructive it can be."

Philip, subbing in for Preston, stopped restocking the hotdog griller and dusted off his take-your-business-elsewhere voice. "If you put stock in anything that woman says, you need your head examined."

Letty rolled her eyes at Philip as the girls took their drinks and fled. "Way to scare off the customers, old man."

"I think you had that part covered just fine on your own." Then he went back to his hotdogs. Just another day in the concession stand at the passion play.

Letty shrugged before moving out of Marco's way and heading back to the deep fryer so she could drop some corn dogs. Who knew fair food would be such a hit at an Easter production? She hadn't believed it when she'd first taken over running the concessions. Sure enough, though. People wanted nachos, pretzels, and deep-fried goodness at the annual production of the passion play. They ate before they went in, during intermission, and on their way back to the parking lot.

As somber as the play itself was, a celebratory mood filled the lobby. It was fitting. Easter wasn't about death. It was about life. Full life. Abundant life. Eternal life. Easter was about the kind of life that was only available in Christ.

A short while later, as the intermission drew to a close and people headed back into the auditorium, she nodded to her crew. "It'll be pretty quiet for the next hour or so. Once the play's over, we'll get bombarded again. Everything will be fifty percent off, and they all know it. We've got to sell as much of the food as we can because none of it will keep 'til next year. Before then, though, we'll take fifteen-minute breaks in pairs of two. I'm on first rotation. Who's with me?"

Janie raised her hand and Letty laughed. "No need to ask permission. Come on. I'm going to pop into the back of the auditorium. Want to come with me?"

Janie nodded, and the two of them headed to the auditorium doors. One of the ushers — an unobtrusive security guard — opened the door for them once they showed their bracelets. They slipped quietly into the back of the auditorium, and Letty led them over to Dawson's sound booth.

Their movement must have drawn his attention because he glanced their way. It was almost pitch black this far back in the auditorium, but there was just enough light to make out the white of his smile before he turned his attention back to his sound and lighting equipment. Even though she'd seen the rehearsal dozens more times than she could count, seeing the full production always sent a shiver up Letty's spine.

That wasn't really Jesus up there on that stage. Those weren't really apostles. This wasn't really Jerusalem. Yet every year, God did something during the Easter production that blew her mind.

This year? The man playing Jesus had come to Christ. Could the world get any stranger? Or their God any greater?

And if what she'd seen and heard was true, God had filled Wendy's eyes with light and hope once again. He'd also done some pretty delightful things in the lives of Bek and Penelope.

As for her, God had brought her peace, the kind of soul-deep peace she'd always longed for. She'd learned things about her father — like his faith — that had changed her entire world. And though she would have happily avoided her mother 'til the end of time, God had seen fit in His infinite wisdom to bring the two of them together. Their confrontations had burned as bright as fireworks, and Letty had fled more than once. In the end, though, God had shown her just how close He'd always been, even when her hurt had made her feel alone. God had also shown her where her strength came from, and she'd learned to lean into that strength like never before.

As she did every year, Letty had been praying that God would move the hearts of the people in attendance. Also like previous years, she celebrated the many ways God worked in the lives of those who gave of their time and talents to support the production. From the moment she'd accepted Christ, God had amazed her, and this year's play was no different. God's grace and love shone forth in the town of Gilead in a special way. It shaped the very fabric of the community. It was the beating heart of the town.

And Letty couldn't imagine living anywhere else.

Which was why, once Easter was over, she was going to meet with Lyla from Delightful Dwellings Real Estate.

It might have taken her a decade to decide, but the time had come to set down roots, and there wasn't a better place anywhere in the world than Gilead, Kansas.

35

"So? Ready to go?" Dawson happily interrupted Letty's work. She was elbow deep in the fryer, and she kept sighing or grunting every few seconds.

She looked up. "What time is it?"

"Closing in on midnight. Where is everyone?"

"I hate keeping the volunteers late on our last night. Every year I say I'm not going to do it, and every year I still send them home before the cleaning's done."

Dawson grabbed an apron from the hook and put it on. "Tell me what to do."

She chuckled. "Pink paisley looks good on you."

He sashayed through the concession stand like he was on a runway. When he got to the end, he turned around and put his hand on his hip in a goofy model's pose. "Now tell me what to do."

She shook her head and turned back to the fryer. "Double-check to make sure everything is unplugged and let me know if anything looks dirty."

He methodically went from one appliance to the next, checking each one over and making sure it was unplugged. By the time he made it back to where he'd started, she'd almost finished with the fryer.

"I'm in awe of you." He couldn't have stopped the words if he'd wanted to.

Letty's head snapped up. "I'm soaked in sweat and covered in grease. It's hardly the time for sweet nothings."

"But it's true."

"You're not half bad, either."

A smile tugged at his mouth, and he let it bloom. "I'm glad you take care not to let my ego get the better of me."

She dumped the last of the cleaning rags into a five-gallon bucket. "Care to haul this to my car for me?"

He flexed his muscles, and she shook her head.

Once she locked up, he held out his hand to her. They walked toward the parking lot, hand in hand if a bit lopsided as he hauled the bucket of wet rags.

"Did you ever picture your future like this?" Letty's words were soft in the stillness of the night.

"What do you mean?"

"Small town Kansas? Was that ever your dream?"

"Truth? No, not quite. There was a time, though, when you were my every dream."

Her steps faltered. "We were kids."

"I know. And I know what I felt back then was at best puppy love. I've never been a fool, though. I make plenty of mistakes, but I know a good thing when I see it, and you, Letty Stanton, have always been goodness personified."

He could imagine her blush. Flattery made her uncomfortable. Too bad he planned on showering her with it for years to come.

"I remember dancing with you that night at my birthday party."

"Oh?" He'd been under the impression she hadn't remembered him at all.

"The week before, there was a football game. An upperclassman from your school had cornered someone from my school. The kid stuttered, and the guy from your school was shoving him around, saying ugly things."

"Brett Washington."

"Hm?"

"The guy from my school. It wasn't the first time he'd done something like that."

Letty nodded, though her attention was clearly still in the past. "The kid from my school had a bad stutter. It wasn't his fault. It's not like there was anything he could've done about it."

"Brett was always on the lookout for a target. If it hadn't been that kid, it would have been someone else."

"You stopped it."

Dawson glanced down and found her eyes focused on him. "I didn't realize anyone else was there."

"I was in the shadows. I guess I've always been most comfortable there." Letty shrugged. "I tried to pull up the police siren sound on my phone to scare everyone away, but you arrived before I got it. You walked right in between them, shoved Brett off the kid, and put an end to it before anyone could throw a punch."

"That was a long time ago."

Letty shrugged. "I saw you defending that kid, and so when you asked me to dance, I said yes. I'd seen you around before at events and stuff, but I'd never bothered to learn your name. I was…"

Huh. And who said good guys finished last? "You were…?"

"I'm not proud of it, but I was pretty self-involved. I didn't see much past my own life."

Ah. Maybe she thought she should have noticed him more

back then. "Aside from the fact that we were both pretty much kids, you had plenty to deal with in your own life. Don't beat yourself up over things that you couldn't have helped anyway."

She shook her head but let the smile escape anyway. "You had a hero complex even back then."

"Hey, if that hero complex got teenaged me a dance with the prettiest girl in town, I'm not going to wish it away."

They reached Letty's car, and she popped the trunk so he could put the bucket of rags in it.

"What do you say? Think I can score another dance with that pretty girl?"

She glanced around the parking lot that held only one other car besides their two. "It's got to be forty-five degrees out here."

"That's practically summer weather up in Chicago." He held out his hand.

"You're nuts." She shook her head but stepped into his arms.

He pulled her close and started humming a song as they moved in sync around the parking spot, her head resting on his shoulder.

"Is that...?"

"*Love You Like a Love Song.*"

Her eyes laughed at him. "That's the song we danced to that night."

"Is it too corny if I say it's been one of my favorite songs ever since?"

"Yes. Definitely too corny."

"Whew. Good thing. Because I totally wasn't going to say that."

Her shoulders shook with laughter as they continued to move in rhythm to the song he no longer hummed.

"Can we keep doing this?" Her voice was soft, tentative.

Letty was a bit of a commitment-phobe. There was no way

she meant what he wanted her to mean. "Dancing in parking lots? Absolutely."

"No. This. You know what I mean. You, me. *This*."

He pulled her in closer and joy thrummed through his veins. "As far as I'm concerned, we're going to be doing this for the rest of our lives. More than this, if I'm being honest, but I didn't want to go too fast and scare you off."

"I guess I do have a history of being skittish."

"Just a bit."

"But I want to keep doing this with you, too." Her voice was stronger this time, no hesitancy in it. "Forever."

No time like the present. Dawson took a step back and dropped to one knee. "Marry me?"

Letty's eyes flared wide. "Um. You heard the part about me being skittish, right?"

He couldn't help the smile that surely split his face. "I don't have a ring, and I'm not asking you to set a date. We'll go as slow as you want. We can wait a decade if that's what it takes. I'll sign the most ironclad prenup you've ever seen so you know I'm after you and only you."

The parking lot lights reflected in her eyes, giving them the hint of starlight. "You're a lot of things, but a gold digger isn't one of them."

"This asphalt's getting kind of cold. And a little damp. You gonna leave me hanging?"

"I don't want it to take a decade, but I don't want to rush, either. Circumstances robbed me of some of my happy memories, and I want to enjoy this. I want to savor this time in my life. And someday I'm going to want to tell our children about when we dated and how magical it all was. I want good stories to tell them."

His heart hammered in his chest. She wanted to have children with him someday. He'd stay on the cold asphalt as long as it took to get a *yes* from her. "Like the night we danced in a parking lot and you agreed to someday marry me?"

She took a step closer. "Yeah. Memories like that."

He cleared his throat. "So, just to be clear. You're saying yes? That you'll marry me?"

"I'm saying yes."

His cold knee protested, but he ignored it, jumping up and pulling Letty into his arms. Dawson hugged her close and whispered in her ear. "I love you."

She pulled back and wiped a tear from the corner of her eye. "I love you, too. More than I thought possible."

Then she wrapped her arms around his neck and pulled him closer. Her lips brushed against his, the lightest of butterfly touches.

He gently cupped her face in his hands and pulled her in for more. Her lips were soft under his as he kissed her with everything he felt. All the yesterdays. All the tomorrows. All the love. All the promises to walk through it together. He poured it all into that kiss.

"Ahem."

Dawson broke off the kiss and glanced around.

Of course it would be him. Mr. Watersby stood over by the third car in the lot. "It might be a good time to head home, don't you think?"

Letty tried to squirm out of his arms, but Dawson held her long enough to kiss her on the forehead. "I'll see you later."

She nodded to him, escaped into her car, and drove off into the night.

Mr. Watersby walked a few steps closer. "Haven't seen Mrs. Stanley around in a while. Any idea what might have her so occupied elsewhere?"

Dawson glanced at the older man. "Why do I think you probably know more than I do?"

The older man tapped his cane on the ground. "I haven't a clue."

Dawson shook his head and answered the earlier question. "Law enforcement says she colored inside the lines just enough that they can't do anything. Plus, statute of limitations, lack of proof, and whatnot."

"But Letty's free of her?"

"Letty never has to see or speak to that woman again unless she chooses to."

"The law might not be able to do much, but her life won't be the same after this."

Dawson didn't usually care for how the wealthy handled things amongst themselves, but in this case, he was glad for it. "Her reputation is shot. She can't stay in San Francisco, and she doesn't have the money to go anywhere else. If I had to guess, I'd say she'll probably try to find someone with money to marry."

"She could change. Turn over a new leaf. Repent."

He looked at Mr. Watersby. "Do you think she will?"

"I pray she will."

Talk about a non-answer. "I suppose I ought to pray the same thing."

"You might not be ready to pray that just yet, but you'll get there."

"What makes you so sure?"

The head of HR shrugged. "Same way I knew you were the right one for the job."

Dawson stared at the man whose keen eyes watched him back. "You're far craftier than you want people to realize, aren't you?"

Mr. Watersby tapped an index finger against his temple. "Always keep 'em guessing."

"I'm glad you blackmailed me into keeping this job."

The older man's car door was open, and he had one foot

inside when he turned back to grin at Dawson. "I have no idea what you're talking about."

Dawson watched him drive off before looking up to the starry night sky.

Thank You for giving me the home I didn't realize I was missing out on.

Despite his protests, Gilead had become home. Even more, Letty was his home now, too.

Speaking of... Mind if I drop by on my way home? I miss you already.

Her reply text came through seconds later. Spending the night at Philip's. Just arrived. You can stop by, but he says I should warn you that his rifle is loaded and in good working order.

On my way. And with that, Dawson started the engine, pulled out of the college's parking lot, and drove toward a future filled with more promise, joy, love, and hope than he ever thought he'd experience again.

THE END

AUTHOR'S NOTE

Thank you for spending time with me in Gilead. I hope that, like me, you have enjoyed getting to know these characters and the community that allows them to thrive.

If you can, please take a minute to tell others about this book by leaving a review on Amazon and Goodreads. I wouldn't mind if you told all your friends about it, too. Or took out an ad in your local paper... although that might get costly. In all seriousness, though, reviews are golden, and I appreciate every single one of them.

As any writer will tell you, gratitude is a way of life in this line of work. I am beyond thankful that God gives me stories to share and the words with which to tell them. He has allowed me to do something I love, and it's a blessing every single day. Writing isn't a solitary journey, though, and I want to thank the people who have helped pull this story together and make it shine.

Thank you to everyone who cheered me on while catching all my dangling modifiers and missing antecedents: Elizabeth Maddrey, Gunnar Grey, Pam Green, Sarah Hamaker, and Janda Sample. You're each invaluable.

ABOUT THE AUTHOR

Heather loves coffee, God, her family, and laughter – not necessarily in that order! She writes approachable characters who, through the highs and lows of life, find a way to love God, embrace each day, and laugh out loud right along with her. And, yeah, her books almost always have someone who loves coffee. Some things just can't be helped.

She takes joy in creating characters that, much like her, are *flawed...but loved anyway.*

You can sign up for Heather's newsletter by going to
http://heathergraywriting.com/newsletter
or catch up with her online at
http://www.heathergraywriting.com.
She can also be found at
http://www.facebook.com/heathergraywriting
http://www.twitter.com/laughdreamwrite
http://www.instagram.com/laughdreamwrite

OTHER BOOKS BY HEATHER GRAY

Informal Romance

An Informal Christmas

An Informal Arrangement

An Informal Introduction

An Informal Date

An Informal Affair

An Informal Reception (coming 2025)

Rainbow Falls (contemporary Christian romance)

Skye

Olive

Sunny (coming winter 2024)

Rose (coming summer 2025)

Other Contemporary Christian Romance

Nowhere for Christmas

Bella Notte

Ten Million Reasons

Ladies of Larkspur (Christian Western Romance)

Mail Order Man

Just Dessert

Redemption

Regency Refuge (Christian Regency Romance)

His Saving Grace

Jackal

Queen